Cover Design by Bill Toth

Book Design by Iris Bass

Cover Photo by Bill Brandt

He Died With His Eyes Open

Derek Raymond

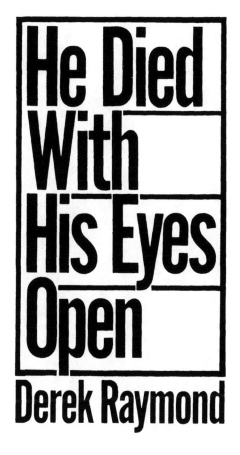

AVAILABLE
PRESS

BALLANTINE BOOKS • NEW YORK

For Fiona

'One eye was shut where he knocked it on leaving the tomb
But the other is staring from behind the cornflakes
On middle-class dining-room sideboards.'
                                        Robin Cook
                                        The Edencourt, 1952

1

He was found in the shrubbery in front of the Word of
God House in Albatross Road, West Five. It was the
thirtieth of March, during the evening rush-hour. It was
bloody cold; and an office worker had tripped over the body
when he was caught short going home. I don't know if
you know Albatross Road where it runs into Hanger Lane,
but if you do you'll appreciate what a ghastly lonely area
it is, with the surface-level tube-station on one side of the
street, and dank, blind buildings, weeping with damp, on
the other. That evening there was yet another go-slow on,
and when I arrived at seven there were people still
massing to get down the tube stairs to the trains, which
were running very rare.

It was pelting with rain on an east wind when I got there.
I found Bowman from Serious Crimes standing over the
corpse with a torch, talking to the two coppers off the beat
who had been called by the man who had stumbled on
him. Water ran off the brim of Bowman's trilby and
dribbled down the helmets of the wooden-tops to end up
in their collars.

Bowman handed me the torch without a word and I bent
over the dead man. His eyes were open—one only
just—the surfaces peppered with the grit that an east wind
hurls at you off London streets. He was wearing a cheap

grey suit with cigarette burns down the front and a tatty
raincoat. He was medium height, with thin hair turning
grey and a boozer's nose, aged between fifty and sixty. Both
his arms were broken, and one leg; the bone poked out
blue through the trouser cloth. His head had been battered
in below the hairline and brains had slopped down his left
cheek into the mud. I got the impression, though, that
despite his injuries he hadn't died at once. In the dull eyes
there was still a flicker of some memory that he meant to
take with him wherever he was going.

When I had finished I stepped back with a last glance at
his face. They had left some of it, I will say, whoever
they were. It wasn't a strong face, but one that had seen
everything and then not understood it until it was too
late. I've seen plenty of violent deaths, but never anything
worse than this one. His wounds were multiple, but not
random. They weren't consistent with a hit-and-run or even
a casual robbery (who would trouble to rob him, though?).
No, he had been systematically beaten by one, or more
likely two practitioners who knew exactly how to do it.
Specialists, you might almost say. Villains, you might
almost say.

'What do you think?' said Bowman.

'I think they weren't joking.'

'They?'

'There must have been more than one. No one man could
have done all this. And wherever it was done, it wasn't
here—there's hardly any blood under the body.'

'Oh, I'd noticed that,' said one of the size nines in a tone
of exaggerated patience. Like all these clever coppers who
wanted to make detective-constable but never did, he had
been moving around sussing things out. 'For my money
he was done in a motor, then he was dragged out here—you
can see the marks in the ground—then dumped to make
him look like a derelict hit-an-run, see?'

'You're a murderer,' said Bowman coldly. 'You're one of

the special kind, a killer that don't want to get caught.
You beat a bloke to death in a motor—blood all over the
fucking place. Next, I'm you. I come round to your place
an I say, can I have a look at your motor, please? Routine
inquiry, sir. Blood everywhere, you berk.'

'I hadn't thought of it like that, sir.'

'I know,' said Bowman, 'so just draw your pay as a
police-constable and try leaving it to us, son. Unless,' he
added, 'you'd like to use your crystal ball once more and
give us the motive?'

'No, sir.'

'Anyway,' I said, 'you can't beat a man to death in a
motor, there isn't room.'

'It could've been done in a truck, maybe,' said the other
copper. Nobody took any notice of him.

'Has the pathologist been?' I said.

'All the mob,' said Bowman. 'Been and gone. We was just
waiting for you, and you took your time an all.'

The nosy copper that Bowman had put down snuffled
with mirth in the dark. Bowman turned to him and said:
'If you've something to say, lad, say it out loud and in
English so's I can give you the answer—you mightn't find
it all on your own.' He said to me: 'What do you think he
was killed for? Money?'

'He doesn't look like the kind of ice cream who ever had
much on him,' I said. 'Do we know who he was, by the
way?'

'Of course we do,' said Bowman, 'we found his papers in
his pocket. Charles Locksley Alwin Staniland, aged
fifty-one.'

'I don't think I'd kill a man for fifty quid,' I said.

'Oh, I don't know,' said Bowman, 'some of these kids are
desperate nowadays. Anyway, you can get going on it
now—it's your case. And don't get in my hair at all, will
you?'

'You haven't any,' I said, looking at his bald head in the torchlight.

There was no love in the look he gave me. He was a chief inspector at thirty-two, only recently bumped up to his rank; he was cheerful, brutal and clever, cheeky and cocksure. 'It's a derelict death after all,' he said with dismissive contempt that implied he had bigger fish to fry over at Serious Crimes. 'We get lots of them.' He looked at his watch. 'Christ, I've got to get back by eight o'clock. I'll be off, then.' He started to walk back to the road, where the squad car with its revolving blue lamp and chattering radio waited at the entrance to the tangled garden. 'The ambulance'll be down to take him away sometime, only as you know—'

'Union's having a go-slow again.'

'In any case,' he said, 'I'm sick of being pissed on by all this rain.'

He didn't care about the rain at all. What he meant was that Staniland was a case with no promotion in it; he would cheerfully have stood under a cold shower for twenty-four hours fully dressed if there had been. The local law notified him of these cases, and as often as he could work it, he turned them over to us to pick up the bits.

At the gateway he turned to me and stood with his legs apart, at ease, his hands clasped behind his back. We faced each other. As I say, we didn't get on, so it was a good thing we were in different departments and didn't see too much of each other.

'You really want to stay a sergeant, don't you?' he said.

'I like to see justice.'

'Justice? You're a berk,' said Bowman. 'You're forty, you're a sergeant, and you actually despise promotion.'

'I'm not on my way upstairs like you are,' I said. 'Not with cases like this one.'

'It won't even be reported.'

'No, I know,' I said. 'And that sort of thing matters to you.'

'Of course it does.'

'But the trouble with you is, it shows.'

'Have it your own way,' said Bowman. 'You can stay on at Unexplained Deaths till you rot, for all I care. Anyway, I'm going. I'm late already.' He dug his chin into the collar of his mac and gestured to his driver to pull up closer. As he was about to get into the car, he turned and said: 'By the way, you'd better call the Factory and I'll have his property sent over to you. There's plenty of it.'

'You've been over his place already?'

'I've had it done. I'll give you the address.'

Well, he was efficient—but I knew that.

'You can leave me your torch while I wait for the ambulance anyway,' I said. 'You won't need it back at the Factory. Not with all that strip lighting.'

He gave it to me without enthusiasm. 'I don't like your manner,' he said. 'You're only a sergeant, but you're cheeky. You reckon yourself, you do. You think you're fast.' He was in the back of the car now, with the window half up against the rain.

'Working where I do makes me feel independent.'

'Don't carry it too far,' he said.

'You can turn your back on me if you like,' I said. 'I wouldn't shoot you with your own torch.'

I just wanted him to leave.

When he finally had, with the blue lamp flaring in the rain and a smazz of pistons and exhaust from the red-striped and white Rover, I sent the two turnips back to the gate and squatted down by the dead man's face again with the torch on. I wanted to see if I could get some line on why the man might have died and how he had got here before the people who knew it all started to try and tell me.

After a while I began to reflect on the withering remarks Bowman had passed on Unexplained Deaths. The fact

that A14 is by far the most unpopular and shunned branch
of the service only goes to show that, to my way of
thinking, it should have been created years ago. Trendy
lefties in and out of politics or just on the edges don't like
us—but somebody has to do the job, they won't. The
uniformed people don't like us; nor does the Criminal
Investigation Department, nor does the Special Intelligence
Branch. We work on obscure, unimportant, apparently
irrelevant deaths of people who don't matter and who never
did. We have the lowest budget, we're last in line for
allocations, and promotion is so slow that most of us never
get past the rank of sergeant. Some of us transfer to other
branches out of desperation, but not many; and of those
who do transfer, most do it sooner rather than later. We
can solve a murder with as much skill as any of the
Bowmans, whatever our rank, pay and pension—the
difference is in our attitude. Just like Bowman, we spend
our time looking into dead men's faces, round their rooms,
into the motives of their friends, if any, lovers and enemies.
But unlike some policemen, we never make excuses about
being undermanned; not do we care if the case we're
investigating never gets into the papers, nor becomes a
national manhunt—and when my friend Sergeant Macintosh
was killed by the man he had trapped in a bedsitter off
Edith Grove last year, there was no posthumous George
Medal for him. No murder is casual to us, and no murder
is unimportant, even though murder happens the whole
time in a city like this.

While I was looking down at the dead man, the two
coppers came back. The eager one that Bowman had put
down looked at me. He was much too clever to say anything
this time, and even when he did speak he wasn't exactly
polite or impolite—he just managed to leave the politeness
out. The other PC, who hadn't annoyed me yet, slipped
up when I asked him to call the ambulance again on the
walkie-talkie, and he called me 'son'.

'Is that what you call your station sergeant?'

'No.' He was a brutal-looking blond of about twenty, who moved about with a controlled restlessness, cherishing his fists. I could tell he despised anyone who was different from him, older than him, cleverer, weaker, or in disagreement with his views of the society he helped to administer.

'I'm about twice your age,' I said. 'Would you like me to call you son, son?'

'No.'

He wasn't suitable to be a police officer. He was much too partial—partial to a battle with 'enemies' of whom he took far too sharp a view. He wasn't the kind of man you could depend on to ensure a democracy. He wasn't a quick thinker, either. The Met was too full of people like him, and it was no good the bosses upstairs saying they had to take what they could get. With three million unemployed, they could get whatever police force they wanted, like they did with the army. But a policeman's job, properly carried out, is much harder than a soldier's—or should be. You don't just obey orders. You have a code, but you are often on your own (I always was) and then you have to invent your orders.

'You haven't been with us long,' I said.

'A year.'

'Just take being a policeman easy,' I said. 'No need to rush at it like a bull at a gate.'

'Okay,' he said. He said it softly and unpleasantly, with a reserved chill in his eyes. I wondered what would happen to anybody he was questioning if he ever made CID, if they gave him a bit of cheek.

'That's all right,' I said. I noted the number on his shoulder-strap. I always noticed those things.

There was an uneasy silence, so I said: 'To pass the time till the ambulance comes, have either of you any comment to make on this case? Anything at all that comes to mind?'

'That isn't our business, Sergeant,' said the brighter
policeman, with the air of having learned a lesson.

'Come on. I'm asking you both.'

'Hard to say,' said the blond.

'Was he on drugs, for instance?' I said. 'You've got what
evidence there is in front of you, same as I have.'

'I wouldn't know,' said the blond, absently. 'After all, I'm
just a copper on the beat. With only a year's service in.'

'You'll never make CID with that attitude,' I said.

'Who says I want to?'

I turned to the other one. 'Why does a middle-aged drunk
end up on a piece of waste ground looking as if he'd been
hit by a shell?'

'He had enemies.'

'Most people wouldn't give a fuck about a poor slob like
this,' I said. 'They might give him a push or smack him
just one. Why a terrible beating like that?'

'Yes, and it was planned. They topped him in one place
and dumped him here.'

'Right,' I said. 'But what motive could they have had?
They took a risk.'

'Yes, okay,' said the brighter police-constable. 'Yes, I'd
buy that.' He spoke with a South London accent that
guttered in his throat like a flame in a cracked chimney.
The other one sulked in the rain on the edge of the
torchlight. 'Well, if they went so far as to kill him, maybe
he knew too much about something. Maybe he was a
grass—a snitch.'

'Maybe,' I said. 'And he might have done bird, but
somehow I don't think so. Anyway, that's easily checked.'

'Or a spy?'

'No,' I said. 'Foreign powers don't operate like that. Nor
do terrorist groups. They blow people to bits, shoot them,
or even run them over. But they don't beat them to death
and then move them. They haven't time.'

'Money, then.'

'It doesn't look as if he had any.'

'Well, it must be one of those three, Sarge. I can't think of anything else.'

'No,' I said, 'nor can I. At least not yet. Not till I've been through his gear, talked to his friends, if any.' I added: 'You've been a help, anyway. What's your name?'

'Marvell.'

Just then the ambulance appeared. It arrived with a groan of expiring sirens, though it hadn't been in any hurry. When it stopped, no one exactly erupted from it. After a decent pause two men in blue uniforms got down from the vehicle in a calm, quiet, British manner. The man who wasn't the driver got the back steps of the ambulance folded down and produced a stretcher which he couldn't manage to make work right away. The man who was the driver walked slowly over to us and remarked: 'Well, here we are.' We were obviously meant to feel that this was in the nature of a revealed truth. He glanced at Staniland's body and said with a knowledgeable look: 'This him?'

'Well, if it isn't,' I said, 'it was.'

'Fraid as he was dead,' said the driver, 'he rather come at the bottom of the list, there being a case of industrial action on.'

'You're right,' I said, 'he was in no bigger a hurry than you are.'

'You'll excuse my asking,' said the driver, 'but would you be trying to take the piss?'

'Well, if I was,' I said, 'there'd be fuck all you could do about it. Now get him on board, or I'll report you for wasting police time.'

There was a very long pause indeed. 'As a police officer, you're supposed to be impartial as to union action,' the driver said.

'And I am being,' I said. 'I'm just telling you to get on with it. What's not impartial about that?'

'You,' said the driver bitterly. His mate said, without

looking up from the official notebook he was scribbling in:
'Okay, George, let's get out of the rain and weigh him off.'
He looked at his watch, noted the time down in his book
and shut it. He said to the two police-constables, 'We'll just
be in time for this new TV series they're running. It's all
about some old king being murdered way back by a lot of
geezers in baggy shorts and funny hats with pearls on.
They all prowl about rabbiting a lot and waving swords at
each other, see, then there's a bloke in a fur cloak has em
all up in court and gives them a long rabbit, then he has em
all topped. It's good.'

'I don't think it's good,' said the blond copper. 'I think it's
a load of crap.'

'You're biased against hist'ry, you are,' said the driver's
mate, 'if you won't mind my saying so, Officer.' As he
spoke, he was shoving the stretcher with the corpse packed
onto it under a blanket into the white interior of the
ambulance. When he had finished he slammed the doors on
it, walked round to the front and climbed in. The driver,
with a choked look, got in too and started up. The ambulance
pulled away at a sedate speed. 'Night, all,' the driver's
mate called back.

Nobody answered.

Inside the ambulance the ruined face of Charles Locksley
Alwin Staniland screamed silently up at its white roof
which a British Leyland operator had sprayed one day when
he happened not to be on strike and needed the overtime.

2

I went to see the police surgeon who had examined the
body on arrival and said: 'What did he die of?'

The surgeon said wearily: 'Everything.'

When I asked the pathologist the same thing, he
said: 'You tell me what he didn't die of, I don't
know.'

'Why don't you know?' I said. 'You're the pathologist.
You're supposed to know.'

'The wounds happened so quickly on top of each other
that it's hard to say which came first. Not impossible,
only I'm not through yet. But you can take it that they
broke the arms and the leg first, also the fingers, and that
the blow that put paid to him was the one to the frontal
lobe of the brain, which was delivered with something like
a builder's two-pound hammer.'

'I wonder how he got himself so well hated,' I said.

'Don't ask me things like that,' said the pathologist, 'I'm
only quite young still and don't have much insight into
people's horrible motives. I hope I never do. Anyway, it's
not my job,' he added. 'I only establish time and cause of
death, and I'm not a copper, I just work for them.' We were
in the morgue, and he dropped a clutch of bloody
instruments into a sterilizing unit. He glanced at Staniland's
blue face as his assistant slid him back into the fridge.

'Maybe he knew too much, sort of overspecialized in something.'

'And then talked in his sleep,' said the assistant, banging the fridge shut.

'Find a builder,' said the pathologist with a snigger. 'Find a hammer, why don't you? I'll match it up to the hair and the blood group.'

He made me rather angry. 'Imagine one day having a girl-friend too many, doctor,' I said, 'and being hammered to death by a jealous lover. Or not a girl-friend. A boy-friend.'

'Look here, I trust you're not insinuating—'

'And imagine us, the law, mimicking Sherlock Holmes over your remains—me, and that assistant of yours with the wisdom of the ages in his face and the dead fag in his mouth.'

3

I went to sleep in my dreadful little bachelor's flat—a police
flat—at Earlsfield after starting to look through Staniland's
property. Bowman had sent it over in an old suitcase. I
dreamed that far below me, under the walls of a ruined
fortress, there was a field faded brown by drought with
rocks lying in it. I was abroad somewhere—somewhere
that smelled—and sitting on a terrace that I suddenly found
was made of rotten canvas. My legs dangled over the edge
and my feet were so far from the ground that the soles
tingled. On either side of me well-dressed people chatted
to each other, unconcerned. Then the whole structure
yawed, swayed and fell devastatingly away; I screamed as
I fell towards the field with the rocks in it. 'They have to
get you in the end,' Staniland remarked calmly as we fell
together, 'otherwise there'd be no end to the pointlessness.'
    I woke up sweating.
    I thought about myself. I'm not a bachelor, I'm divorced.
On the face of it, that doesn't mean much in the police
nowadays; if it did, they'd never be able to fill the ranks.
    It doesn't help your career, though. The people upstairs
have never been divorced, whatever they may have done
on the side (things that come out, to the public amazement,
from time to time).
    Having accepted yet again that I would always be a

13

sergeant, I stared upwards into the dark trying to focus on
Staniland, trying to imagine him walking, upright and alive,
without his injuries. I went on trying to picture him like
this until I wished morning would come.

I switched the light on at five and got out one of the tapes
from Staniland's collection and put it on my cassette
player.

> People stroll about in Battersea Park among the
> dogs' turds as if they had all time before them. I
> hope they really believe it—they might as well.
> They go round and round the park, then they turn
> about and go back to the flats which border it.
> There they sit and worry about their problems and
> wait for the pubs to open. In spite of their
> clothes, a lot of them are sitting tenants and on
> social security. If you tell them that you're a
> writer, they tell you that they are writers too,
> though they haven't an ounce of talent in them,
> only resentment and nastiness. They come on very
> liberal: this is false. The moment you have anything
> interesting going in your room—a discussion, a
> party, a screw—they start banging on your floor
> with a broom handle like a jealous mother-in-law in
> a hopeless, elderly way. These are your 'neighbours'.
> Next evening you see them in the bar of the
> Princess Caroline wearing secondhand snappy
> coats, sporting gold buttons with anchors on them
> and peaked caps at an angle, Lenin-style. They
> look ready to denounce anybody; they are obsessed
> with their middle-class status right down to the
> last assumption, down to the mongrel which they
> strain against their feet in their balding suede
> bootees just as if these snappish animals had a
> pedigree. When I have had a few drinks these
> people turn into predatory birds, hornets and wasps.

If I criticize them, they tell me I have no pity. If I
do not, they have none for me.

Under its strictly tended foliage, the keepers of
Battersea Park shut the gates at ten-thirty at night,
reminding you that you aren't in the country now,
while not three streets behind the Rastafarians
roam and howl. Shut out of the pubs down there by
unwritten law they rule the streets—their prey the
Asians, those whites who are too defenceless to
retaliate and, in general, intelligent-looking and
therefore possibly rich people. The only things the
jobless blacks can call their own are the paving-
stones. Battersea is representative of a hopeless
national situation, and only a succession of typical
British governments could ever have got us out into it.
I loathe Battersea. I just want to go mad.

I turned the tape over, but the other side was blank.

4

Morning came. It shone through my uncurtained bedroom window, but I still listened. I came to a grim account that began:

France. The moment I got back to Duéjouls after the others had left, the first thing I did was burn all my daughter's clothes—all her books and toys that had been left behind. As I couldn't bear to look at them I took everything up behind the house into the courtyard and made a huge fire of them. It was August, and the heat was so great that I was afraid everything would catch fire—the house, the whole village, the sky. I watched her books burn up: *Ant and Bee*, *A Busy, Busy Day*, *Mister Clumsy* and *Mister Clever*. Her drawings of houses and cats and snails soaring over her impression of the house on the wind wrinkled and flared; the flames gusted through them. The evening breeze from the *causses* flailed and tossed her works lightly up to heaven, as lightly as if they had never been. I felt horribly faint inside as I stoked the fire—as if I had been transformed by a fever that left only my twisted body behind, listless and hideous. I knew only that it had to be done as I burned her clothes and shoes; it was the cost of my failure as a father

16

and a man. Everything would have to be explained
and paid for—but not tonight, not now.

Wine now: I drank the cold wine from the bottle
while the fire burned, destroying our past for us,
my daughter's and mine. When the fire looked like
dying of exhaustion under its ash I threw some
eau-de-vie on it and raked the slabs of half-burned
paper and material with a hoe they call a *harpe*
round here to give the fire more air. When everything
was burned I knew I had done right as I reeled
away. I knew Charlotte could never, and would
never, come back. Life had never permitted her
any fairy-tales, not with me as her parent: and it
never would. I cried with fury and despair and
loneliness as with a last gesture I threw on her old
gumboots and school satchel, and burned her
exercise books with their drawings of frogs and
flowers, and the scraps of poems she had copied
out with Madame Castan:

'*Jamais, jamais, tu ne la rattraperas!*'

I have to explain what the agony of her loss
means—she was my heart, my soul, my other
self. But I could never possibly have told her so,
and so I lost her. Once I knew I was going to lose
her, I suddenly preferred to lose her at once, not
wait. I rushed onto the loss. I sent everybody
away, then went away myself. Ah, existence is like
water, it is everywhere and yet it flows away.
They say I have Polish blood on my mother's side.
When I came back, as I had to, I burned everything
that had belonged to her. Are the English inhuman?
While I was in England my brother said I
shouldn't take everything so seriously. But if you
don't take love seriously, what do you take
seriously? Belongings? Money? Property?

    I put the fire out in the evening. I wonder how much of this I can really stand?

After a pause on the tape Staniland answered himself:

    Only so much, of course. I'll find out when the time comes.

He had found out all right. I put Staniland's tape down on the floor. I wondered how much Bowman, or the two PCs, or the pathologist, or anyone else, would have understood of them.

    I wondered how much I really understood.

5

Bowman had given me the wrong address for Staniland. It wasn't the Battersea address on the national insurance card they had found on him, but the one on the letter from a bank saying they'd be really very glad if he'd drop in pretty well at once and see them about his overdraft. It was dated only a fortnight before his death, and the address it was sent to was in Lewisham, the clock-tower end of it. I had found the letter mixed in with his papers.

I started to think about everything I knew of Staniland so far, beginning with his being smashed to pieces. He was fifty-one. He was balding. When they washed the blood off him, he had nice hands (you could see from the one he still had the shape of) and had perhaps been attractive to women. Too attractive? But he didn't read like a love-'em-and-leave-'em specialist. The fingers on that hand—his right—were stained with nicotine. He was a drinker, too—you could tell that from his nose, and from his problems, as shown up in what he had recorded. Not an alcoholic, though; his handwriting was too precise, the letters as a rule well-formed for a man who had written quickly, and well-spaced between the lines, the lower loops never entangling themselves with the upper loops of the line below. It was an educated, reflective, intelligent hand that didn't go with the cheap suit he was found in.

What the hell had the man been doing?

Bowman hadn't found any money on him. He was on welfare. That didn't mean he was broke, though; plenty of people these days fiddled the rules; they had to, to survive. Besides, there was the letter from the bank—he must surely have had money in it once, even if he only owed it when he died.

I kept shutting my eyes till it was late enough on in the morning for me to go out and get information, trying to visualize Staniland and how he had lived. A writing man. A self-confessed failure, tortured by the loss of his daughter. A man who had lived abroad, probably for a long time (I should have to listen to all his tapes to verify that, but there were so many of them that it would take time), an educated man.

I rang Bowman and got him at home just as he was leaving for the Factory.

'Staniland,' I said.

'Well?'

'Why did you give me that address in Battersea when he lived in Lewisham?'

'I didn't know I had.'

'Surely you knew the address where your blokes had picked up his gear from,' I said. 'His papers and tapes and so on.'

'Why? Is it interesting?'

'You're a cold-hearted bastard,' I said. 'What he taped you could listen to for a thousand years and have no pity for him.'

'Cut out the Shakespeare,' he said. 'I've got a conference at ten for a million-pound breaking-and-entering. Anyway, did I play any of them? Did I have time? You're joking.'

'I'll make you wish you never had,' I said, 'if I don't get better cooperation from you than this.'

'Are you threatening me?'

'Yes,' I said. 'Less of the casual cut and thrust, slap and

tickle—more dedication to fact, like we learned in police college, week two.'

'Okay, okay. Is that it?'

'It is this time. But we're supposed to be one solid force. That's why it's called a force,' I said. 'And the next time you just throw any old unverified blag off on me over a case I'm handling, you might just have a stumble on your next flight to the top.'

He said incredulously: 'Are you telling me? Me? A chief inspector?'

'Yes, I'm telling you,' I said. 'Murder outranks rank, so watch your step.'

'Why don't you watch your blood pressure, Sergeant?' he said, and put the phone down.

I looked at the dead receiver for a while.

Before going out, I thought some more. It wasn't a routine killing—not a skinhead rolling and mugging job. Hatred—evil that Staniland had evoked in someone—had caused those deliberate, frightful injuries. Earlier in the morning I had heard on one of Staniland's tapes:

> You can go on for a long time explaining what life means to people, but do you still not understand that you're never going to get out of this alive? The question is, though, how are you going to die? Everyone has to face that. The problem is, how to do it consciously, deliberately, plan it up to the last moment, and record everything. The best thing would be if I could record what happened at the last moment, and after that moment. But someone else will have to fill that gap—if it's ever filled.

I played that part again. For a moment I wondered if he meant suicide. But however Staniland had met his death, it certainly hadn't been that way. Besides, I didn't think that that was what the passage meant. I reviewed what little I

knew; the salient point was that he hadn't been killed
where he was found. He couldn't have walked. It always
came back to murder.

As if by telepathy, the pathologist rang.

'I've done the autopsy.'

'Well?'

'His blood group is O negative. . . . Look, what I really
want to say is that he was even worse hurt than we
thought when he came in. Both legs were broken, not just
one—a fracture of the left kneecap, he couldn't have
walked on it, as well as the multiple fracture of the right
tibia. There's bruising to the medulla too, something I
missed at first. Dislocation of the left shoulder, third and
fourth ribs cracked on the same side.'

'Christ, what did they do?' I said. 'Drop him from a
building? An aircraft?'

'No, no,' said the pathologist, 'it was a beating all right.
I'd say you were still looking for that hammer, though the
ribs and the kneecap might have been a kicking. Someone
had a go with a knife, too; there's a long gash up his right
arm that would have had to be stitched. So, hammer, knife
and the boot—there would have had to be at least two of
them, you can bank on that.' He stopped for breath.

'Anything else?' I said.

The man coughed. 'Well, lab tests show that he didn't die
very quickly.'

'I'm listening.'

'They started with the fractures at the extremities, the
fingers and hand, then the legs. Then he was hit in the
right eye—it was nearly closed, you remember—there was
extensive bruising. Then there was the knife wound. It
looks to me as if it was thrown, the knife. Probably a
flick-knife or kitchen—heavy, at any rate—say a twelve-
centimetre blade. They, er, rather worked him over.'

'What actually killed him?'

'Oh, the blow to the brain, frontal lobe, without a doubt.

Loss of consciousness aggravated by extensive bleeding.
The fractures, shock. Then coma and death. That's all. I'm
getting my report ready for the coroner now.'

'Thanks, you've been a great help.'

'No I haven't,' said the pathologist, 'so don't try and fool
me.'

'All right, I won't.'

'Come round any time you feel I can't help you some
more,' said the pathologist. He was young, like he said,
and laughed in his nose the way people do when they feel
they've made a terrifically good joke.

I put the phone down. I felt sick, as if I had taken the
beating. I put my head between my knees till the greyness
in front of my eyes stopped and the buzzing in my ears
cleared. I'd listened to hundreds of pathologists' reports,
but none of them had ever affected me like this.

When I felt better I found that I had been staring at a
page of Staniland's writing that I must have kicked aside
with my foot where it lay on the floor. It was in a dreadful
ballpoint scrawl and read: 'I never ever want to see
Barbara Spark again, she's bled me to death. My heart's
empty, my brain's empty, she laughed at me the last time
I had an orgasm.' The next paragraph must have been
added later; anyway, it had been written with a different
pen. 'How can anyone so beautiful be so bloody? How can
any love as intense as mine die against this ice?' There
was a scribbled footnote:

> It makes me feel as if I were a woman writing like
> that, or Barbara herself—a tart, frigid with guilt or
> terror, wanting sex and loathing it simultaneously.
> Has my passion turned me into her? What are you
> trying to do, Charlie? Destroy yourself? Don't tell
> me you planned this! Death, yes—but love, passion,
> jealousy of a passing footstep in the street outside,
> this consumption of the blood, never. Fifty-one,

fifty-one, and clowning to hide your grief and
rage! You can't satisfy her? How can you satisfy a
beauty that vanished as you entered it?

The clown falls on his nose to a burst of laughter.

It's ridiculous to say that he showed signs of a disintegrating
personality, I thought; the man was perfectly sane. He was
too sane, even.

I got a Nicholson's street guide out from under a pile of
books in the corner and pinpointed the address at Romilly
Place where Staniland's bank manager had sent the letter.
Then I got up and tipped everything that was in the
battered suitcase which contained all that was left of
Staniland out onto the floor. Underneath the masses of
paper there were eight more cassettes. I picked one up at
random and put it on. A hasty, troubled voice which I
realized must be Staniland's said:

'Oh, God, I want to fuck you!'

And a woman's voice replied wearily: 'Must you use that
word? Why are you such a bore, Charlie?'

There was a scream of agonized tape and nothing more
on that side; I took it off, but not before I had played it
over a few times more. Distressed though it was—and
probably not sober—Staniland's voice was like his
handwriting, intelligent and direct.

I put on the other side of the cassette. Staniland said:

I had a bad night in the Agincourt again; the
Laughing Cavalier was in as usual. He always has a
go at me, but I drink until I don't care. What does
Barbara see in him? I see her looking at him when I
glance at her in mirrors; she drags on a cigarette
and gazes at him without expression from under her
fat white eyelids, her legs crossed on her stool,
sensuous and neutral. I'd do anything, *anything*, to
keep her out of the place. But if she decides she

wants to come that's the end of it—you can hardly argue that a girl who works the clubs should keep out of a public house.

Later, after a pause, he went on:

I've just come in from the Agincourt. The Laughing Cavalier didn't touch me, although I provoked him again by tying him down in a discussion about class. He took the piss, surrounded by his mates as usual. But he didn't touch me—there was only that time, a month ago, when he smacked me about with the flat of his hand out in the yard behind the gents. 'You going to the law about it, then?' he said when he had finished, stepping back. 'No,' I said, 'I'm going back inside for another pint. You sure you've finished?' 'I'll finish you for good one of these days,' he answered, turning away.

Earlier in the evening, Barbara had been in the pub with me. But she got fed up around a quarter to ten and left, saying she was going over to a club. Before she went, though, the Laughing Cavalier came up to her and put his arm round her waist, with me right next to them, daring me to do anything about it. He does it quite often, offhand, but it's enough to wake dreadful pangs of jealousy in me. Does he do it because he fancies her? Or simply because he hates me and wants to needle me?

He's a horrible man—meaty, big. He's got a face like a lorry-driver who wants to overtake everything on the road. He's forty or so, and has orange hairs on his thick arms. When he's finished putting his arm round Barbara, treating me as if I weren't there, he lets go of her laughing, and gives her a friendly push on the shoulder. She shrugs, and all

his mates laugh too, taking the tone from him.
Then somebody buys a round and they all go over
to the fruit machine. Afterwards I ask Barbara
why she lets him put his arm round her like that;
she shrugs again and says, why should she mind?
I say, because I mind. She answers, then you
should do something about it (smothering a laugh),
if I'm your girl. But afterwards, back in our room,
she says she's sorry. I say: 'Sorry for me, you
mean?' 'Yes.' 'Can we make love, do you think?' I
say, getting undressed. 'Depends,' she says. 'What
on?' 'Could you get it up?' 'I don't know,' I say,
'I've had a lot to drink. I could get it up in the
morning, though. I always can.' 'I never feel randy
in the morning,' she says. 'What I'd really like
now is a cuddle, Barbara.' 'Buy yourself a teddy-
bear, then.' 'No, I need to be cuddled by you,
badly; nobody but you will do. I love you, and I'm
pretty frightened of life just now.' 'I know you
are, Charlie,' she says, 'and it shows.' *What a
courtship*, I think. 'I'm too old for you, Barbara,' I
say. 'Poor Charlie, I'm afraid you are. I only liked it
with you when you used to tell me things, when
we just used to lie side by side together in the dark.'
'But it isn't enough for me, Barbara, only lying
there beside you. I love you too much; I love you
with all my being.' 'All right, come on, then, let's
see what you can do, if it'll keep you quiet.' After a
while: 'Well, there you are, you see, Charlie, look,
you can't do anything.' 'I'm trying, I'm trying, just
let me try once more.' So I do, and I *can't* get it
in, and there's a long silence from her while I'm
trying and a sigh or two, and then in the end she
says: 'Well, it's hopeless, Charlie. Come on, get off
me, face facts.' 'It's the man in the pub, Barbara,'
I say. 'What about him?' 'I can't seem to get him

out of my head while I'm trying with you.' 'Are
you frightened of him?' 'He hates me.' 'Don't
provoke him, then, Charlie. Then he won't go for
you.' 'If I didn't provoke him, then he'd know I was
scared of him.' 'He knows anyway.' 'I don't know
why, but he gets between my love for you.' 'Go to
sleep, Charlie. Please.'

So I go through the motions of falling asleep. I
am in agony. Even to talk to myself about it like
this is agony. I stare into the darkness all night,
with my back towards Barbara, my cock lying
useless in my right hand, trying not to let anything
show.

I switched the machine off and picked up the street guide
again. Tapes? What do tapes mean in a court of law?

6

The Henry of Agincourt public house was in the middle of Greenwich Lane, and very antique it looked, too, compared to the high-rise blocks that surrounded it. A few West Indian heads hung glumly out of the windows in ballooning Rastafarian hats, and three men in jeans were watching a fourth dig a hole in the pavement to the strains of a tranny. The pub had painted medieval wooden beams at the front, and the sign displayed the monarch after whom it was named. He was wearing a large crown, a doubtful piece of armour and an expression of quiet, or possibly drunken confidence, and was peering up the road as if he had just seen a lot of Frenchmen. Someone very thin with a pointed iron hat on stood humbly beside him, trying to get his bow and arrow to fire, his metal foot planted on the word BEER.

Inside, the place was built entirely of concrete, which nevertheless bore signs of attention from various demented customers. The bar was narrow, and behind it stood an unbelievably disagreeable-looking stout man, who had to be the governor. It was only a quarter past eleven in the morning; however, as I came in, he was helping himself to a triple vodka, obviously not his first of the day. Someone had recently cut the side of his face open, and the wound still had stitches in it. Apart from ourselves, the place was

empty. When the governor saw me he started to shake
violently and gulped off the vodka, setting the glass down
on the counter with an uncontrollable slam.

'What'll it be?' he said wearily.

'I'll have a pint of the Kronenbourg.'

'It's off.'

'The other stuff, then, with the long German name
there.'

'It's warm.'

'I don't care, I'll have it just the same.'

'Not if I don't feel like serving you, you won't,' he said in
a threatening tone. He picked up a pint glass all the same,
but had a good deal of difficulty holding it still under the
tap. As it was, he didn't fill it quite to the top, and when
I mentioned this he opened the tap full on with a furious
gesture, causing another pint to go roaring down the
drain.

'That's for the ullage,' he remarked with mystical
satisfaction, and pushed the glass across to me. He added:
'That'll be eighty-five pence.'

'Seems a lot,' I said, giving him a pound.

'A lot of what?' he said, glaring at me. 'A lot of beer, a
lot of money, or a lot of fucking cheek?'

'A lot of money.'

'Look, if you don't like the price,' he said, 'why don't you
just drink it up and piss off?' He flexed his mottled
forearms in their shirt-sleeves. 'You'd be well advised to.'

'When I've asked you some questions maybe I will,' I
said. 'I'm not knocked out by all the excitement in here, I
must say.'

'Questions?' the landlord repeated in a tone of disbelief.
'Questions? In *this* pub?'

'That's right.'

'The only people who dare ask questions in this pub,' said
the governor, 'is the law, and even they don't bother
overmuch.'

'Really?' I said. I produced my warrant card. 'Well, funnily enough, fancy that, I am the law.'

'Oh, Christ,' he said. He sank his forehead into a wobbling hand. 'I knew there was something about you. You're all I need. What is it this time? The punch-up we had in here Saturday night? There was only one geezer got badly cut besides me, and he didn't want to prosecute.'

'It's nothing to do with that. It's about a man that was found dead last Friday night, and it turns out he used this pub a lot.'

'That don't tie me into it!' shouted the governor, taking a step backwards.

'I didn't say it did, I didn't say it didn't.'

He screwed his eyes up tight and opened them; they were red and blue, like dartboards. 'I need another drink,' he said. 'How about you?'

I shook my head. 'This man's name was Charles Staniland,' I said, when he came back with it.

He took a long swallow. 'Gotter show a profit,' he muttered, 'got to. Otherwise the brewers, they get uptight. An showing a profit here means I don't never know the customers by their names. Not down here. You'd be mad to,' he added with a ghastly smile. 'Mad!'

I was getting restless with him. 'You won't show a profit if you don't cooperate with me,' I said, 'for the simple reason that you won't be here. One word from me to the boys over at Lewisham and bang goes your licence—we'll find a way.'

'Oh, Christ,' he said. 'All right. You got his photo?'

I pushed over a shot taken of Staniland dead.

The landlord focused on it unsteadily, taking his time. 'Yeah,' he said at last, taking a quaff of vodka, 'that's Charlie all right. Made a mess of him, didn't they? Aven't seen im in a while, though, must be three or four days.'

'Of course you haven't,' I said. 'He was in the morgue.'

'Yeah, well, that accounts for it.'

'You're right,' I said, 'that's the sort of date you're bound
to keep. Heavy drinker, was he?'

'Whew! Heavy? What, him? Not half!'

I was studying some words done in burnt poker-work
behind him, above the cash register. I read: 'We'll fight
em up, we'll fight em down, We'll fight for King, and fight
for Crown. We'll stand and fight em till we die—But
they'll NEVER drink Old England dry!'

I felt the landlord was an example of this truth, if of no
other. 'Any idea what he did for a living?' I asked.

'Now look,' said the landlord, 'if I was silly enough to ask
my customers things like that, I'd get some very funny
answers, any one of which could put me in hospital for a
month.'

'He have any enemies?'

'Enemies? In here? Cor, I should think so! Practically
everyone in the place hated his guts. Rabbit on? I never
heard anyone rabbit like he did. Charlie Staniland? Gor, I'll
say!'

'Plenty of people rabbit in a pub,' I said. 'That's what
they're for. Why pick on him, do you think?'

'Well, I don't do that much thinking,' said the landlord
after some reflection. He turned his back on me to refill
his glass. 'Ah, fuck, there's no ice again, never mind. No,'
he resumed, 'thinkin don't pay in this trade, I don't find.'

'But if you did think.'

'Ah, well, if I *did* think, then if I did think about it, then
I daresay I might think that is face just didn't bleedin
well fit. Not that there was anythin particular about the
way he looked—he just looked as if he might've bin
happier up west somewhere.'

'Well, that's where he was found, as a matter of fact,' I
said, 'only rather far out—Acton way, West Five.'

'Ad to be found somewhere, I suppose,' said the landlord.
'Funny sort of bloke, he was. Funny sort of voice, sort of

upper crust, really. Stuck out like a sore thumb at a
wedding, a voice like his did. Odd he's gone, though.'
   'Why odd?' I said. 'If nobody liked him?'
   'I don't rightly know,' he said. 'I never thought of it until
now, of course. I only ad to bar him the once, and that
was because he was that pissed he started to upset the other
customers, and in particular a party of gentlemen that
wanted to discuss something quietly in the corner there, a
private matter.'
   'Anyone hate him enough to kill him?'
   'Oh, come on, now,' begged the landlord, 'even you can't
expect me to answer a question like that.'
   'It's a lucky thing for you you haven't got orange hairs on
your forearms,' I said, staring at them. 'Any of your
regulars got them? Big? About forty? Sometimes known as
the Laughing Cavalier? Fancies himself with the birds?'
   'Not that I know of,' said the landlord. He tried to
answer absentmindedly, but he looked more as if he were
about to cry.
   'Okay,' I said, 'well, we'll stack that one.'
   'What do you mean, stack?'
   'Put it on one side. I've got plenty of time. I can always
come back.'
   'Look, let me tell you, Sergeant, we're law-abiding here. I
run a tight house.'
   'I can see it's tight,' I said. 'But the law-abiding bit—that
could improve.'
   'I'll tell you everything I can,' he said pleadingly. 'Just
give me a chance.'
   'Here you are, then,' I said, 'let's try this one. Who was
his friend?'
   'Friend?'
   'Girl-friend. He use to come in with a girl-friend.'
   'Ah, *girl*-friend!' he said eagerly, as if immensely relieved.
'Oh, *her*. Who was she, you say? Christ, I don't know. I
remember her, though. Dark, thin, buck teeth.'

'No,' I said, 'I happen to know from the dead man's tapes that she was big, nice figure, had long blond hair, and gave him a hard time.'

'Oh, sorry. Yes, that one. Yes, I get you now.'

'Do you?' I said. 'Lucky for you. Because you could find yourself in a bit of bother if you didn't look out. I might decide I wanted to wind you right up tight if you misled me, just to see what would happen. And do you know what would happen, fatty? You'd go off pop! Like that.'

'Okay, okay,' he said.

'What was her name, now?'

'I don't know. Could it've bin Barbara something?'

'That's the one,' I said, 'that's the one. And what was her surname again?'

'I'm not sure, I think it was Spark.'

'I think so too,' I said. 'Very good! I'll buy you a drink if you go on like this. Okay, then. Did she use to frat with anyone in here except Staniland? Any of your customers?'

'Not to my knowledge,' said the landlord heavily, pursing his lips. 'Not to my knowledge.'

'Look, I'm going to give you an insight into police thinking,' I said, 'a sort of treat for your being so good. When someone I'm questioning exaggerates a gesture the way you've just done, then I know for a fact he's lying. So I'll just remind you of that bit about cooperating with me again, okay?'

'Look, no one went anywhere near them,' said the landlord desperately. 'Honest. No one in here liked either of them, see?'

'It's funny, but that doesn't square with things I know.'

'What do you know?'

'Nothing you need to.' I continued: 'So you're sticking to that are you? That everyone in here just stood off at a distance and went no further than take the mickey out of him. You prepared to swear to that?'

'Oh, that's right! You couldn't single no one out, like. No special person in particular. No, you couldn't!'

'Strange,' I said, 'strange. Doesn't sound typical of a villains' incubator like this at all.'

'Well, that's the way it was.'

'And you've no idea why people took the piss out of him. Apart from his accent.'

'That's the truth.'

'And yet some person or maybe more than one hated him so much that they did this to him.'

'Yeah, it certainly looks nasty.'

'That's an understatement. You do fully realize this is a murder I'm investigating?'

'Certainly I do!' said the landlord wholeheartedly, 'an I hope you catch them bastards what did it to him. Poor old Charlie!'

'We'll catch them,' I said.

Behind me the pub was beginning to fill up: men drifted in two, three at a time, truck-drivers mostly, the hole-digging gang from the street.

All at once the landlord jumped. 'Oh, do leave!' he urged me in a deafening whisper. 'If those two over there even suspect I've been talking to you, they'll have my guts for a garter.'

'All right,' I said. But I was in no hurry. I finished up my warm beer at my own speed. 'But I'll be back, I'm afraid.'

'When?'

'You won't know when. It could be any time.'

'Look,' said the landlord, jerking the till open with a backward flap of his hand, 'I wonder if I could make a contribution to the Police Orphans' Fund?'

'Certainly,' I said. 'You just send the cheque to the Fund at Scotland Yard. The address is in the book.'

'That's not what I meant,' blubbered the landlord. 'I mean, oh, don't tie me into it, please.'

'Fuck off,' I said.

I watched him crawl off down the bar.

As I left I looked hard at the men who had so agitated the landlord. The first was quite small, but that didn't make him harmless. He wore custom-built jeans, a red sports shirt, and a fawn cardigan; his gold wristwatch was too big, like his ego. A fat wallet stuck half out of his hip pocket, daring some poor idiot to have a go. He was talking to another man with protruding front teeth, wearing a yellow anorak, black jogging pants and sneakers. Neither of them had orange hair, and they weren't big. But they were villains. I couldn't remember their names offhand, but they were a team and liked clubs best of all—a nice slab of cash punctual on the thirtieth of the month for protecting a club or else smashing it up. They saw me looking at them; I didn't care. They were making casually for the bar as I left.

Outside, the first edition of the only remaining evening paper had come out on the streets. I got one. Someone called Lord Boughtham had just been appointed Foreign Secretary and had made a long speech in the Lords that criticized everybody but himself. That was one way of earning sixty thousand a year.

There was nothing about Staniland in the paper. Staniland wasn't news.

7

I sat in my office at the Factory reading Staniland. It's called the Factory by the villains because it has a bad reputation for doing suspects over in the interrogation rooms; people who still think our British policemen are wonderful ought to spend a night at the Factory banged up or put under the light by a team of three. We call it the Factory, too: but, if you want to know, it's the big modern, concrete police station that controls the West End north to Tottenham Court Road, south to Hyde Park Corner, northwest to Marble Arch and east to Trafalgar Square. The building itself is in Poland Street bang opposite Marks & Sparks.

I stopped reading for a moment and started thinking about the cassette that had prompted me to go over to the Agincourt. I had played it over at home several times more. Out in the passage the cleaning lady had her transistor radio on while she slopped the water about; a lot of trendy lefties started protesting about something, and she switched it to another station.

The landlord had been lying—not that that surprised me. He lied because he was frightened; that didn't surprise me, either. It needed a man with better nerves than his to run that place, also someone who wasn't a total pisspot. I wondered just how badly Staniland had been beaten up

36

outside behind the gents there—probably much worse
than he had let on. The landlord had certainly been
threatened and told to button it, very likely by the two
villains who had passed me drifting towards him in the bar
that morning.

I would have to go back there at some point. I wondered
vaguely what I should wear for the encounter, and
couldn't decide between a Chieftain tank and a self-
propelled gun.

I put one of Staniland's tapes on again. He said:

> There's a point where the string of the balloon
> breaks and it glides upwards to burst at that height
> where shape is no longer possible for it. Meanwhile,
> to be an animal that thinks persistently in terms
> way beyond its lifespan sets us a frightful problem.
> Every day you amass knowledge in a frantic race
> against death that death must win. You want to
> find out everything in the time you have; yet in the
> end you wonder why you bothered, it'll all be
> lost. I keep trying to explain this to anyone who
> will listen.

There wasn't any more on that tape, so I went on to the
next. They were in a dreadful muddle, gaps, bits erased,
some inaudible because used twice. His papers were
scribbled over in the margin with footnotes and remarks
on the back. He seemed never to have used a typewriter.
In some places the handwriting was well-formed and
-spaced; in others it was hasty, with tremors, almost
illegible.

This piece was a letter. The handwriting was not
Staniland's, but it resembled it; only it was much more
careful, stiff. There was no address at the top, and no date.
It read:

Dear Charles,

I have been thinking over our telephone conversation
the other night, and have regretfully decided that it
isn't the slightest use your coming over here and
expecting any sympathy from us now. You chose to
go abroad and live there for years at a time, never
writing, letting all your contacts drop; and now that
life has gone sour on you, you start ringing up or
coming over and telling us all your woes. It won't
do, Charles. Betty and I have enough problems of
our own. I know you want money, though you
don't say so outright, but I saw it in your eyes
last time you were over here and I could hear it in
your voice—I'm not your brother for nothing. I'm
afraid it's no good. Even if I gave you money, you
would only fritter it away on drink or on one of
those awful women that you get so hooked on. No.
You've simply got to understand that there's a
code in life, and no foolish thirst after knowledge
and experience will compensate you for abandoning
it. Either you follow the code, or you don't. And
you haven't. I hate putting this so bluntly, but
you leave me no choice.

In great regret, believe me, and of course love,
your brother G.

P.S.
You can stay the night, of course, any time; I know
Betty will be delighted to make up the spare bed for
you. But that's *all*. I'm sorry you've come to this pass,
old boy, and I honestly wish there were something
I could do. But my own business is in difficulties;
in fact, at times I hardly know where to turn.

With a brother like that, I thought, no wonder Staniland
drank. Rereading the letter, I thought there came across a

vague note of envy, as though 'G' were attempting to
punish Staniland for some experience which the brother, to
his vexation, had never had.

I turned the letter over. On the back Staniland had
written the single word 'Crap.'

As I was gathering up his papers to put in my desk
before going to lunch, a single sheet of his writing,
smaller than the others, fell out on the floor. It read:

> I understand everything now, Barbara. It was I
> who was so stupid; I should never have started to
> detect lies in people. Too late I've discovered that
> if you strip people down to the truth, you give them
> no chance to survive. Lies and evasions are
> necessary; they give us a chance to dodge.

An advertisement cut out of a highbrow economics review
was pinned to the sheet. It was highly unoriginal and
showed a man in a business suit, carrying an executive
briefcase, apparently about to tread on a wristwatch that lay
in the foreground. The blurb read: 'Man is as beautifully
crafted as the best Swiss watches—a Masterpiece that even
Time can't beat!'

Underneath Staniland had written: Balls.

On the sheet behind the advertisement the letter continued:

> Every time I write or talk to you, Barbara, it's like
> my blood flowing away. My words leave my mouth
> only for you, like blood leaking out round a
> dagger. Once I've spoken my brain feels grey and
> feeble. Please come back to me—stay with me. It
> won't be a life sentence for you. I feel myself
> moving towards something final that even the
> dimmest of us will be able to understand. Oh,
> Barbara you are the only—

There wasn't any more, just a brown circle where a glass of whisky had probably stood.

Before going out I rang Bowman's office, but they still hadn't managed to trace Barbara Spark, they said. I got the impression they hadn't tried very hard and weren't going to, and realized that I would have to do it myself.

8

That evening, around six, I went and interviewed Staniland's brother. It hadn't been difficult to trace him as, unlike Barbara Spark, he was in the telephone directory—Grampian D. Staniland. I could have rung him but decided not to, and simply went round. He owned a nice little bit of listed property in a Victorian terrace behind Essex Street Market. It was a fine April evening when I approached the purple front door with its shiny lacquered knocker. The street was bathed in petrol fumes and peace, except for a group of young blacks who were sneering at passers-by and drinking Coke against some railings; they gazed at me expressionlessly as I went up and banged on the door. There was no answer at first, so I banged again and lit a cigarette. Just as I had got it going the door opened with a lot of rattling and went a short way back on a chain. I couldn't see anything except a hand on the door; it seemed to be a woman's hand.

'Mr Grampian Staniland's?'

'Yes,' said the woman, still invisible, 'I'm Mrs Staniland. Who are you?'

'Police.'

The dim blur of her face appeared, scrutinizing me. I identified myself and said: 'Could I see Mr Staniland, please?'

'I don't know. I suppose so.'

'I'm afraid I've got to see him.'

'Oh, well, you'd better, then.'

She undid the chain. 'There,' she said at last, half
opening the door. 'You can come in.'

I squeezed past her into a narrow hall and managed to get
past two tables loaded with knick-knacks. The hall was
festooned with objects—paintings in gold frames, three
clocks, an owl or something in a glass case, and a good
many swords crossed on the wall and hanging there by
means of strings. I avoided putting my elbow through a
picture of an enraged-looking officer in a busby, but hit a
suit of armour which crumpled rustily into itself.

'What is this?' I said. 'An antique business?'

'It's my husband's private collection,' she said frigidly.

'I wouldn't care to have to pay death-duties on it.'

She didn't like that. She got in front of me and strode
carefully into the sitting-room. I looked round it. There
were more sofas there than in any small room I had ever
seen—four. There wasn't logically room for anything else;
all the same there were more pictures, either landscapes
with the shrubbery done like overcooked sprouts or with
that military flavour again. Also, eight small piecrust tables
crouched under the weight of heavy shaded lamps,
figurines, silver ashtrays and beaded mats meant for standing
drinks on. Sombre curtains half shrouded the windows
and were looped back with silk ropes. It was much too hot
in there.

Now I could take Mrs Staniland in. She was not
attractive. She took no care of her skin, which resented it
in the form of wrinkles. Also she had no bottom, and was
flat all over like a playing card. Her gravy-coloured tweed
suit did nothing for her, and she did nothing for it back.
She had a nice string of pearls on, but they only
emphasized the fact that she had no bust. Now that she had
got over the shock of the word 'police', she spoke

in a harsh, upper-class voice, some of it copied.
Once she tried smiling, but it didn't get very far.

'What is this about?'

'I'd rather tell Mr Staniland that, if you don't mind.'

'I see. I'll go and get him, then. Wait here, please.' She
began swinging her skirts grimly towards the door.

'Just a minute,' I said. 'Would you mind my asking where
all this gear comes from?'

She gazed at me as if I were something that shouldn't
have been on the carpet (a Shiraz, I noted automatically).

'Most of it was in my husband's family. He inherited it.'

'They must have needed a castle to house this lot.'

'They had one.'

Well, she had got me there.

'I can assure you it wasn't stolen,' she add viciously, 'if
that's what you were getting at.'

'I wasn't,' I said. 'It just makes rather a contrast with your
brother-in-law's life-style, that's all.'

'Oh, God,' she groaned, 'you haven't come about him,
have you?' She added: 'You know, I had a feeling. Well?
What has he done now?'

'If you'd like to fetch Mr Staniland for me,' I said, 'you'll
find out.'

'He's collating some incunabula upstairs.'

'Ask him to come down, please.'

She started to leave, reluctantly.

'It's all right, I won't whizz anything,' I said.

She slammed the door on me. While she was gone I
gazed at the seven clocks in there with me. One had a
little pendulum that jumped up and down; another hiccoughed
when it got to the half hour but couldn't chime. I wished
they would upgrade our wages so that I could buy some
decent clothes; I would have looked slightly less out of
place.

Somewhere upstairs I could hear two voices going
vigorously in counterpoint; the sound was followed after a

while by the sound of four feet galloping energetically downstairs. Then the door flew open and Grampian came in rubbing his hands, also wearing a tweed suit—a well-cut one, two hundred and fifty pounds' worth from Savile Row.

'Good evening to you,' he boomed heartily. 'My wife tells me you've come about my brother Charles. Well? What has he been up to this time?'

'Well, he's gone and died,' I said.

That put an end to the heartiness; there was a sudden silence in the stuffy little room.

'Died?' repeated Grampian. 'Good God, whatever of?'

'Of repeated blows from a builder's hammer. He was beaten to death.'

'Who by?'

'That's what I'm trying to find out.'

After a while Grampian said: 'I very much doubt if we can be of any help to you. There was very little contact between Charles and ourselves, you know.'

'Really? Well, I have to follow up every lead.'

'Of course you do. Of course.'

'Anyway,' said Mrs Staniland in a brittle voice, 'he was definitely murdered, was he?'

'Oh, yes,' I said. 'We're quite sure about that.'

'Perhaps you could be more explicit,' said Mrs Staniland.

'He just has been,' said Grampian.

'Well, it wasn't an accident,' I said. 'He didn't fall or get run over by a passing car. He wasn't killed where he was found, either. He was found one side of London and he lived on the other.'

'He could have had business where he was found.'

'Most unlikely. Besides, there was hardly any blood under the body.' I produced the photograph I had shown the governor of the Agincourt. 'A bit of a mess, isn't he?'

Grampian took a quick look at it, belched, put a hand to his mouth and said, turning white: 'Please put it away.'

'What exactly were your relations with your brother?'

'Well, hum,' said Grampian, rubbing his hands together, 'few and far between.'

'The further between the better, in fact,' said Mrs Staniland.

'I see. Why was that?'

'Money,' they replied simultaneously.

'He was often asking you for it?'

'Well, he'd have done it even more often if we'd given him the chance,' said Mrs Staniland acidly.

'I assume, though,' I said, gesturing around me, 'that when you inherited all this, er, stuff here, your brother must have been left something too?'

'That's a private matter, I'm afraid.'

'Nothing's private to me,' I said flatly.

A silence fell.

'I wonder if we oughtn't perhaps to ring our solicitor, Grampian,' said Mrs Staniland suddenly, 'if this interview is going to turn awkward?'

'I wouldn't bother him at this stage if I were you,' I said. 'I haven't bitten you yet.'

'No, quite,' said Grampian. He said to his wife: 'I honestly don't see the need, Betty.'

'I just don't like answering questions like these without expert advice,' she snapped. 'That's all.'

'Well, no solicitor on earth can prevent me putting the questions to you,' I said.

'Of course not,' said Grampian. 'It would be fifty pounds simply thrown down the drain, Betty. You must see that. In any case,' he said to me, 'there's absolutely no way we can be implicated in my poor brother's death, don't you see?'

'All right,' I said, 'well, let's pick up the thread again, then. When you inherited, your brother inherited.'

'More than I did, too. He was the elder.'

'So he was quite rich at one stage.'

'Oh, not badly off at all, not at all. Even after duty had been paid. Property, mostly. He had some nice things, too.'

'You're in the antique trade?'

'Oh, I don't know about *trade*, exactly. I dabble in objects, buy and sell occasionally, invest in certain painters and manuscripts a little, yes.'

'What happened to your brother's property?' I said. 'Where did it go? He hadn't a light when he died, as far as we can make out.'

'Well, it's, er, all quite complicated,' said Grampian. He cleared his throat, twice. 'But actually I've got it, you see.'

'Perhaps you wouldn't mind enlarging on that.' I suddenly understood why Grampian's house was so full of things.

'Well, the trouble with Charles,' said Grampian, 'was that he was always roaming about. Never bought a house. Hated settling down. Never had much idea about money, never had any money. So, well, I put it to him—'

'You offered him cash for the lot.'

'That's right,' he grumbled, 'and the hell of a business I had raising it like that in a hurry, too. What with sky-high interest rates—'

'How long ago was this?'

'Oh, I don't know, must be five years or so, I suppose.'

'What was the sum involved?'

He huffed and puffed. 'Oh, pretty hard to remember now, at this distance in time,' he boomed, blowing through his purplish lips.

'Have a go,' I said drily.

He sucked in air judiciously. 'Well—shall we say in the region of thirty thousand pounds?'

I realized instantly that Staniland had been badly cheated. I knew that from what I had seen in this place. But to cheat someone in that way unfortunately isn't an indictable crime, and even less so between brothers.

'What happened to the money?'

'How should I know?'

'What we do know,' Mrs Staniland interrupted, 'is that it went.'

'But you don't know how.'

'That's right.'

'And then he started trying to borrow money from you?'

'Yes, after he came back from France.'

'And how long ago was that?'

'Oh, about two years. After his wife and daughter had left him.'

'Anyway, you neither of you lent him any money.'

'Grampian had told him *all along* that it simply wasn't on!' shouted Mrs Staniland.

'We've got our own row to hoe,' said Grampian, 'and making ends meet isn't easy these days, Sergeant.'

I knew that.

'And then to have him coming down on us!' Mrs Staniland's voice trailed indignantly away.

'But he didn't become unpleasant in any way? Threaten you, anything like that?'

'Oh, no,' said Grampian. 'He just rang up sometimes, came round once or twice—'

'Always drunk,' Mrs Staniland put in.

'And asked for a loan?'

'Well, talked round it.'

'Seems normal enough,' I said, 'if you're a brother who's fallen on hard times.'

'He never fell on any other times,' said Mrs Staniland, and snorted like a horse.

'Did you ever help him at all?'

'Well, I tried to advise him, naturally,' said Grampian.

'What sort of advice?'

'Does that really come within your purview, Sergeant?' said Mrs Staniland.

'It certainly does,' I said. 'We're talking about a murder, believe it or not.'

'I hate your manners,' said Mrs Staniland. 'I find them really detestable.'

'The truth's no respecter of drawing-rooms, madam,' I said.

'If I could just resolve the little impasse,' said Grampian, clearing his throat. 'We were talking about advice. I said to Charles, ease up on the sauce, cut back on these harpies you go in for, that sort of thing. If he'd had a few bob to spare, I could have given him some tips on the Stock Exchange, of course, but as it was—'

'If only he hadn't always been so drunk!' said Mrs Staniland.

'There, there, Betty,' sighed Grampian, '*de mortuis*, etcetera. Poor old Charles.'

I saw how greatly they had both hated, even feared, Staniland; but, like all egoists, they couldn't afford to admit it in case it damaged their own view of themselves in the eyes of a third person.

'Talking of the dead, by the way,' I said, 'there'll be the funeral, of course, after the inquest.'

'Oh, quite.'

'And the expenses.'

'Yes, but well, that's just the snag,' said Grampian awkwardly, snapping his huge pink fingers.

'I don't see how we could think of coping,' said Mrs Staniland firmly. 'Not financially.'

'Yes, we'll have to see,' said Grampian in a tone which suggested that he already had. 'Incidentally, was there evidence that he was drunk much of the time, not just when he came to see us?'

'Some.'

'Yes, well, that was what I was always warning him about, of course.'

'Quite. But, in talking to him, you must have realized that he had other problems, surely?'

'"Other problems?' said Grampian. 'What do you mean?

Mental problems? You don't actually mean to say he was
mad, do you? Do you? Really, how very interesting!'

'No,' I said, 'I don't mean to say he was mad. Quite the
opposite. I just mean there was evidence to show that life
had got rather on top of him.'

'We could all of us complain about that,' said Mrs
Staniland tartly.

'What evidence, anyway?' said Grampian.

I hadn't read all through Staniland yet, so I just said: 'A
good deal, and there's more to come.'

'There's always more to come with someone like my
brother-in-law,' said Mrs Staniland bitterly.

'You can't tell me, either of you, what he was doing while
he was in France at all?'

'I've no idea,' said Grampian. 'Just existing, I should
think. Drifting along.'

Just existing. This long, boring London evening,
interviewing Staniland's next of kin, suddenly got up my
nose. I had an image of Staniland himself, somewhere in the
South of France, appearing at his local bistro, hanging
over the bar at six o'clock like a thirsty angel.

'Which would be pretty typical of him,' said Mrs
Staniland.

'He was living on this money you gave him in consideration
of, er, what he sold you?'

'I assume so.'

'All right,' I said, 'what about his wife, now?'

'Margo, you mean?' snapped Mrs Staniland. 'Margo was
nothing but a tart.'

'Still, I gather she had a daughter by your brother-in-law.'

'Charlotte? Destructive little devil,' said Mrs Staniland.
'The only time she came round here with her mother she
broke one of my Delft vases.'

'Oh, well, children do that,' I said. In a flash, I saw my
own child, lying asleep and flushed on a spotless white
pillow. She would be twelve now.

'They do if you don't watch them,' said Mrs Staniland,
'and give them what-for now and then. Thank God I
haven't got any.'

'How did you know your brother-in-law's wife was a tart,
by the way?' I said. 'Just by looking at her?'

There was an uneasy silence, during which the pair
looked covertly at each other; the sun came and went in
slow yellow bursts of hysteria beyond the heavy window
curtains. The pendulum of the little clock I had noticed
before jumped desperately up and down, like a decoy trying
to distract my attention.

'Well, it rather goes back,' said Grampian, clearing his
throat, 'to before.'

'Before what?'

'Well.'

Now the silence was really loud. It was like the lull
before a first flash of lightning.

'Come on,' I said.

'Well, I met Margo in a club,' said Grampian.

Mrs Staniland exploded: 'She was a whore, just a
whore! She worked in night clubs!'

Grampian turned a nasty colour, red and purple. The
colours looked all right in a tweed suit but were alarming
on a face.

'He's just a poor old goat,' said Mrs Staniland hoarsely,
turning away.

'Now, now, Betty old girl!'

She didn't say anything, but put her wrist over her
mouth and started screaming at him from behind it.
Grampian darted me hopeless glances, as much as to say:
We're both men, old boy!

I took no notice. I leaned against a table covered with
bric-a-brac and left him to settle her down if he could. He
managed to get her up onto a sofa, dashed out to the
kitchen and came back with a damp cloth which he
smacked onto her face. She screamed even louder, snatched

the towel away and threw it on the floor. Grampian
picked it up again and put it back on her face, leaning on
her this time to stop her getting up. The table I had
settled my bottom against creaked loudly. He heard that all
right. 'Not that table, if you please!' he shouted politely
above the din. 'It's quite valuable!'

I stood upright, just looking through them, thinking
about Staniland. Mrs Staniland eyed me from time to
time from under her wet towel. As soon as she realized
there was no mileage to be got out of me, she came to her
senses surprisingly fast and sat up little the worse for wear.

'I must apologize for that,' said Grampian.

'Apologize?' she shouted. 'You dirty old man!'

'Now, now, Betty! My wife's a very highly strung
woman,' he confided to me, aside.

'Now, now, my foot!' snapped Mrs Staniland. 'Our
marriage nearly broke up when I found he'd been going
with her. *Very* nearly.' Grampian might as well have been in
Edinburgh for all the notice she took of him. He went and
stood by the door looking sheepish, wringing the towel
nervously in his rosy hands.

'Did your brother-in-law know anything about all this?' I
asked.

'Pah,' said Mrs Staniland, 'who cares? I shouldn't think
so. But I'll tell you this much, Sergeant, do you know
how I found out about it?' She stabbed a sharpened finger
at him: 'He talked in his sleep.'

'Look here, Betty!' said Grampian. 'Now really—'

'Oh, yes you did!' she shrieked. 'Don't you remember
how you used to mumble that she wore nothing but a
fur coat and gilt slippers when she came to you? And opened
up the coat over your face? And didn't you love it? And
didn't you spend a thousand pounds of my money on her,
you filthy old goat?' She turned to me and said calmly: 'We
sleep in separate rooms now, of course.'

'Was your brother running her?' I asked Grampian.

'No, she did it off her own bat,' he mumbled. 'I'm sure she gave him the money I gave her.' He twisted his fingers till the knuckles snapped: 'She loved him.'

'Love?' shrieked Mrs Staniland. *'Her?'*

'Well, she joined him in France with the child, anyway,' I said. 'But what matters to me is, does either of you happen to know where she is now?'

'She's the sort that moves around,' said Mrs Staniland grimly.

'Okay,' I said, 'well, I think that's all. For the moment.'

'What do you mean,' said Mrs Staniland, sitting up straight, 'for the moment?'

'Well, I've got other people to interview, and you never know—a lot more'll come out once we really get digging.'

'Nothing that might redound to our discredit, I hope?' said Grampian anxiously. 'I don't think my wife and I could stand it if . . . I mean, we've told you things between these four walls that . . .'

'Is it going to get into the papers?' said Mrs Staniland. 'That's what I want to know.'

'I couldn't possibly tell you,' I said coldly. 'I don't know.'

'God, I shall really scream if it does,' said Mrs Staniland. 'Now, now, Betty!'

I squashed the cigarette I had been smoking into one of the eleven silver ashtrays. 'Well, I'll be going,' I said. 'If either of you leaves home, would you notify your local police station, please?'

'Er, quite,' said Grampian. They followed me dumbly with their eyes as I squeezed my way out of the room. As I reached the front door I heard Mrs Staniland saying behind me: 'God damn Charles. God damn him!'

That was one way of talking about the dead.

'As for Margo,' she continued, 'I hope she goes to jail, the little slut!'

Grampian said: 'Now, now, Betty, don't you think you ought to take two of your pills?'

'If you weren't completely impotent, Grampian, I wouldn't need any pills!'

I slammed the front door behind me to indicate that I had gone; when I got out into the street I breathed in a very deep breath, then expelled it right out from the bottom of my lungs.

9

Looking through Staniland's things, I found a postcard in a woman's handwriting. The card bore a faded view of some Italian beach but a British stamp, and was postmarked SW3. It started: 'Let me know, Charles, when you are *truly* sorry. Then perhaps we can talk.'

Sorry? I thought. The man was a walking wound, a mobile case of sorrow. The woman's remark, whoever she was, was not merely inapposite but absurd: to require Staniland to feel regret or remorse for what he was amounted to telling a man with terminal cancer that he looked rather ill.

The card continued: 'It will of course, Charles, only be a *talk*. There can, as you yourself must quite realize, be no question whatever of a return to the past.' The card was signed with a self-conscious squiggle that reminded me of an ageing virgin trying to shake an impertinent finger out of her knickers.

Staniland had sensibly annotated the card: 'What balls. Any return to the past would be as improbable as it's uninteresting. "L" had no past—she tried to use mine instead: a self-satisfied old cow of about my own age who introduced herself to me on the beach at Rimini. She had few ideas unconnected with her money, and I tweaked her nose for it one night after dinner.'

The next thing I got out of the pile was a pasteboard card
for a minicab firm called Planet Cars with an address in
the shabby part of the West End towards Euston Road.
Underneath I read the words: 'High Class Cars, Distance
No Object, Theatres, Weddings, All Functions Attended.
Also Vans, Trucks to Five Ton & Artics, Helpful
Drivers.'

There were three phone numbers at the bottom of the
card, and I saw no reason why I shouldn't try one of
them.

10

'E ad a wife, you know.'
  'Yes, I'd heard.'
  'And a kiddie.'
  'That's right.'
  I was taking my ease today, being invited to relax with
the boss of Planet Cars. The office was on the second
floor of a dingy building behind Charlotte Street, sandwiched
between a Pakistani restaurant called the Allahabad,
European and Indian Dishes, and a delicatessen that
specialized in tinned mangoes, chillies and ladies' fingers.
The bow window we were sitting in peered out at a rather
alarming angle onto a public lavatory, kept permanently
locked against queers and youths who wanted to give head
or shoot up in there. Behind this urinary redoubt was a
pub called the Quadrant, in which the Factory took a
permanent interest.
  Around us, at desks in the room, were three startlingly
white girls, two of whom looked adoringly at their boss
while the third read the *Standard* and did her nails. Also
there was an Irish accountant, the first I had ever seen,
doing the drivers' figures with the aid of a computer
terminal, and the whole area was sprinkled with bilious
green telephones which didn't often ring—if one did try,
the call was instantly cut off by the adorers and transferred

to the overworked dispatchers' office on the floor below.
From that floor I could hear voices drifting up through
the thin planks. The day dispatcher groaned on to his
underlings about the shortcomings of fucking amateurs,
while out of the window I could see the only roller-skater
the firm had. It said Planet 209 in black and yellow on his
back, and he swept to an easy stop in front of the office
with a practised double eight, relinquishing the boot of an
SS 100. I watched him take off his skates and make for the
stairs, his satchel for documents booming off his muscled
buttocks, his swatched blond hair swirling against his hips.
'New set of needles today, Dave,' I heard him call out to
someone. 'Twenty bleedin quid!'

'We like to entertain the law,' the boss of Planet was
saying to me. 'Oh, yes, we ain't got nothin to fear from
the law.' He was a small man whose tailor, having measured
him for a little suit, would have charged him the price for
a big one. He evidently didn't care about things like that,
being more interested in the bottle he was pulling out of
his desk drawer. 'Come on, Sarge, just a little one,' he said
in a confiding tone. 'Chivas Regal, ha, ha, Chivas Illegal,
the lads call it.'

'Well, if it really fell off the back of a truck,' I said, 'it
might as well go the distance and on down your throat.
Nothing you can do about Newton's third law. But not for
me, thanks.'

'Newton's,' he said reflectively. 'Newton's. I worked as a
driver for them lot of bastards once. Little firm up by
Finsbury Park there, where you throw a left on Seven
Sisters Road by the underground, you know the scene.'

I knew it. Although I had asked him not to, he poured
some of the nectar into my glass just the same, so I
picked it up.

'Well, here's luck,' he said, drinking. He looked at me
more closely. 'Funny, you don't look like just any old
size-nine turnip to me, you look like you'd got brains. Call

me Tony,' he added, 'you might just as well. Tony
Creamley's the name. If ever the law fires you, why not
come to me for a job; you look as if you'd had some
practice with a jamjar, ha, ha.'

'Easy,' I said, 'that kind of joke tires me out rather fast.'

'Oh, yeah,' he said, 'sure, okay. Nothing diabolical
intended, Sarge.'

'Nor taken.'

'Luckily,' he said. The phone beside him rang and he
answered it, waving an adorer aside and staring absently
out of the window at a tramp trying to have a pee unseen
on the pavement while chewing philosophically on a dead
matchstick. He soon got tired of the voice I could hear
quacking into his ear and said: 'No, you want Creamley
Cars, darling, that's five oh one double three double four.
This is Planet, son.' He listened for about three seconds
more with his eyes shut and said: 'Now, don't give me a lot
of blag—if you're not happy with your Creamley account,
get in touch with their manager, that's what he's paid for. I
should know, my boy pays him, sometimes, ha, ha. On
your bike, get lost.'

He slapped the phone down, turned to me, and said:
'Some people are born to moan, aren't they, born to
moan. Now, Creamley Cars,' he added proudly, 'that's my
son's—that's Clive's own outfit. Three Rollers c's got on
the strength, three Mercs an a couple of bran-new four-door
BMWs. Nice, nice little leasehold in Cannon Street.' He
sighed. 'Smart lad, my Clive, bright as you like, 'n idle as a
whore on a Monday morning—all he thinks about is goin
off to Greece where he's layin this bit of local shirley
temple. Yet c's got this sweet little business, pays off
better'n any bird and it don't talk back—sweet's a nut, right
under his feet, I set im up, I should know. E works the
City, see, we works the West End here at Planet. Mind,
there was the time he tried to muscle in on me, did Clive.
"At least," I says to im dignified, "leave your old dad the bit

where Planet got started." No—e thinks e's a ard man.'
He shook his head; it wobbled like an oyster on the end of a
drunkard's fork. 'Mind, Clive knows what's good for im,
which side the old bread's buttered. Don't e, Eileen?' he
said, looking over at one of the adoring girls.

'Oh, yes, Mr Creamley,' she glittered, adoring away like
mad.

'That's how we operate here at Planet, see?' said Creamley
with satisfaction. 'All one happy fambly, get it?'

'I'll bet!' I said.

'I don't play rough anymore,' he said, sucking his lips.
'No need, see? Not nowadays. Wait till they go into
liquidation. Buy em up, don't rough em up, that's my
motto. That's why you don't see no firm but Planet round
here anymore. Not round here. Mind you—'

'Mind you,' I said, 'you're talking to a copper.'

'Christ, so I am,' he said, smacking his forehead, 'it's
funny, you don't come on like a copper somehow; you
must be either a good one or a fucking bad one. Anyway,
this boy you're here about, I know him from this snap of
yours, that was Planet Two Four.' He took a deep draught
of his Scotch and looked reminiscently at the photograph
between us. 'I can recognize him, just,' he said, 'but Christ
they din't half carve him up.' He exhaled and nodded
introspectively several times.

'My time's the taxpayer's,' I remarked, 'so I'm always in a
hurry. I don't know who pays you for yours.'

'Oh, that's the punters,' he said. 'I've got all my time, I've
won it before I've got up.'

'Bully for you, Tony,' I said. 'Can we get back to Two
Four?'

'Oh, sure.' He drew a bead on a French spotlight with his
forefinger. 'Not much of a driver, Two Four—always
behind with his rent and his drops. Didn't know how to
present himself to a customer, neither. Nor the motor. I
asked and asked him, went down on my bleedin knees, but

e wouldn't even wear a peaked cap and dicky for a
wedding. I said to him: Look, you know how it is, Two
Four, you gotter say lick your arse, sir, touch the hat, bit
of the abdabs, morning madam, fine day, carry your bags,
then stick the old hand out for a bit of the dropsy. But
no, Two Four wasn't into any of that. We ad some right
complaints about Two Four back ere at the office. First
off, I recall, e'd got this big old banger rented him, a
Renault 16, so e got a few airport jobs—e'd race out to
Heathrow, undred mile an hour, frighten the punter half
out of is wits. Mind, the geezer always caught is plane—
usually with a bit too much time to spare for is liking. E
used to leave em gaspin, did Two Four. But e wouldn't
chat em up the way you've gotter if you want a good tip. I
mean, they're only business cunts and that; they only
want to be made to feel they're somethin special while
they're on their way out to the plane, don't cost the driver
fuck all to feed em a bit. Other way round: the driver scores
an the punter thinks, that firm Planet, they've got a bit of
class. But no, Two Four'd only talk to the punters who
din't wanter talk, and even then it was all about France
an such. Yes, we lost a few nice accounts down to Two
Four; folks used to ring up an complain to me personally
something rotten.'
  'A bit eccentric.'
  'I don't know what that word means,' said Mr Creamley
frankly, 'but anyway, in the death we ad to get rid of
him. Busy afternoon it was too, a Friday. This woman
come stormin' into the dispatchers looking for Two Four.
"Where is he?" she says to Smitty. Threatens him, like. He's
only a young lad—Brownie and my head dispatcherine,
ugly bird with a *Harper's Bazaar* voice, were off on the river
ooze. "Where's who?" says Smitty. "Well, you call him
Two Four," she says, "but I know im better as my
husband." Dreadful state she was in, cryin an er face all in
a mess. Pity—she wasn't a bad-lookin tart at that; I'd ave let

er ave One Eight and the 220D (though not Three Three an the Roller), all on credit. "E's gone off with some whore," screams this bird, "is little kiddie and I aven't seen im for a week, I've ad no money from im an I'm at my wits' end." "Look," says Smitty, "I've got work to do, I've got four phones ringin here case you can't ear em, missis, an the rest of the mob as fucked off." E was only obeying firm's orders, see? A lot of our drivers don't use their right names—we do all cash here at Planet, an the last thing a driver wants is to work is cogs off an still get done by the Inland Revenue. Also, you get a lot of funny folks come lookin for the drivers, ex-girl-friends, creditors, writ-servers an the like, an some of em don't half tell artful stories. Anyway, come to a rub, Smitty sends for me—I'd bin listenin in over the intercom anyway. I din't really fancy avin to deal with this boiler; I'd bin playin dealer's choice all night up at Whipps Cross. My ead felt like a bladder flattened between two bricks an I'd a mouth like St Pancras Station. So I sent for two of the van drivers (we do a nice van ere at Planet), One Seven One an One Eight Five, they're from Mile End and fairly heavy, an I ad em give er the arries. But not before she'd gone ahead screamin as ow she'd find im, she was is missis an all, an what was e gointer do about supportin the kiddie an all.'

'You see him again?'

'Two Four? Not a chance. One of the drivers, Four Nine probably, marked is card and that was the end of that. It's a story we've all heard before ere at Planet. You'd be surprised how many of the drivers ave their little problems. And,' he sighed, 'don't we all, my life?'

'Okay,' I said. 'Is that all?'

'That's all.' He burped with difficulty, rubbing his hands across his wiry stomach. 'Too much eggs is very bindin, Sarge, don't you find? But I got this passion for em.'

'You want to get out and about more.'

'Ah, fuck it,' he said, 'I don't greatly care for walkin, not
when I can ride, what's the use? I never was a great one
for the plates of meat, not since the army. An since I was in
the cats meats gaff a year back for my piles, I find
walkin any distance brings a pain on you know where.'

'We've all got a pain somewhere,' I said. 'It's this case
with me.'

'Yeah, well, I'm sorry about Two Four,' said Mr
Creamley, 'I really am. E wasn't so bad. I used to ave im
up to my place at Epping to teach my youngest girl to speak
proper. She ated him. I used to get im out of there in
the death, give im a Scotch, push im a ten, an tell im to
fuck off—"You'll never get a place like this, Two Four," I
used to tell im, "not with its swimmin pool an all, an in its
own acre of ground." An they liked im ere, the lads did,
even if e did rabbit on a bit.'

'This woman that came in,' I said. 'You don't know her
name, I suppose?'

'Well, yes, funny you should ask that,' he said, 'she left
it, I think. Delia love,' he called over to an adorer, 'get me
that woman's address out of Two Four's file, will you?'

Eventually Delia came across with a piece of paper and
stood holding it uncertainly between us.

'Well, go on, darling,' said Mr Creamley, winking with
impatience, 'give it to the gentleman, e won't bite you.'

He looked at it with me. 'Christ, there's even an address,'
he said. 'Fancy!'

I got up. 'Thanks a lot,' I said.

'Any time. Always a pleasure to see the law. Nother drop
of the Illegal?'

'Not today,' I said. 'I'd rather have a cab in a hurry. You
can trust me; the taxpayer always pays cash.'

'Don't I know it,' said Mr Creamley sickly. I left him
rubbing his belly again with a shiny hand.

I tried the address they had given me, but needless to say
she had moved.

11

'It really is a dreadful nuisance his dying like this,' said Staniland's bank manager. 'He had an eleven-hundred-pound loan account, don't you know, and there's the interest owing on it.'

'An unsecured loan?'

'Well, not quite—there are a few equities. But equities are performing miserably at the moment, as you probably know.'

'No, I don't own any shares,' I said. 'I don't know.'

'The bank stands to be several hundred pounds out on this affair,' said the manager. 'Several hundred.'

'We're talking about a murder.'

'I daresay. Even so, it's very awkward.'

He was small and pink, and at first sight looked too young to be a bank manager. He had a harassed expression and a smile that was meant to be nice. He produced it with the practised ease of a conjuror.

'Head office cleared the loan. But I was against it.'

'Oh? Why?'

'Not a very stable individual, Mr Staniland.'

'Did he tell you what he wanted the money for?'

'No. Or rather, he told me some story or other, but I didn't believe it. I don't think he did himself.'

'Did he borrow all the money at once?'

'No, he borrowed five hundred; then, three months later,
another five. I reminded him how steep the charges would
be at today's rates, but he said he was going to be earning
so that that didn't worry him.' He coughed. 'It worried
me.'

He opened Staniland's file, and I looked at it over his
shoulder. 'Most of the cheques are drawn Self, you see.
He drew the entire loan amount right down to this very last
payment for three hundred a week ago. We let it go
through, though it overdrew him, but that was when I
wrote to him—'

'Yes, I've seen the letter,' I said. 'It was with his
property.' I got out my notebook. 'I'd just like to take the
details of these cheques. I suppose you can tell me the
banks they were cleared through? You know the codes.'

'We're not really supposed to do that, you know.'

'No, I know you aren't. But this man was actually
murdered, Mr Bateson, and I am rather keen to catch the
people responsible. I appreciate that you don't want to get
yourself into trouble with your head office, but speed is
vital.'

'Oh, yes,' said the bank manager. 'Oh, very well, then.'

12

Staniland's room was one of the most putrid I
ever saw. I should have been round there already, and I
would have gone if Bowman's people hadn't covered it.
Romilly Place was off the Lewisham end of the Old Kent
Road near the clock-tower; the houses were three-storey
tenements and filthy. It was a dangerous bloody district
too, especially for someone like Staniland—what we call
mixed area, a third unemployed skinhead, and two-thirds
unemployed black. It was a cul-de-sac, and in the warmth
of the spring evening the air was filled with screams as
kids and teenagers raced round the wrecked cars that
littered the pavement. There were about twenty houses,
mostly with broken windows and vandalized front doors.
Some idiot on the council had had the idea of putting a
public callbox on the corner; it now contained no telephone,
no glass and no door—a directory leaf or two skittered
miserably about in the breeze. The house I had parked by
had been gutted by fire; the front had been shored up
with timber, and there were sheets of corrugated iron where
the windows had been; the chimney toppled inwards at a
ridiculous angle to the blackened masonry. A youth saw me
looking at it and came up. He was only about seventeen,
but he had a very old face like a concentration camp inmate.
There was a faint stubble on his long whitey-green skull

that a flea couldn't have hidden in. 'Six geezers cindered in there,' he informed me, and added: 'But they was all black.'

'I'm looking for number seven,' I said.

'It's the one behind you,' he said, 'but everyone's fucked off. They say one of the ice creams that lodged there got topped over Acton way.'

I could have asked him how he knew that, but I would have lost him if I had. It would have made me smell of law, and I wasn't in a district where the law gets much cooperation. So I said: 'Oh, yeah? Well, I'm just looking around.'

'Why?'

'For a room.'

'What, in there? You must be bleeding mad. The place was rotten with fuzz only day before yesterday. You on wheels? That Ford over there? The Escort?'

'That's right.'

'They don't half go, them Escorts. Got a player in it? Any good tapes? You like to take me an my mates for a ride?'

'What's in it for me?'

'Well, I could get you into number seven easy, see, if you wanted to squat.'

'Yeah, that's what I wanted,' I said. 'For four of us. Looks nice and cheap.'

Some more youths had gathered round while we were talking. I let the skinhead pick his team for the ride, then ripped them round Lewisham clock-tower a few times.

'Where you get this jam?' the skin said enviously when we got back, walking round it. 'It's nice. You nick it?'

'What the fuck's that got to do with you?'

'All right, all right, dad—no need to go bleedin bananas.'

One of the youths standing around said: 'I could get you into that house if you wanted.' He hadn't been asked on the clock-tower trip; he was Asian, though I knew from his accent that he was South London born. 'You want to shoot up, dad?' he murmured. 'Pot? A sniff?'

'Why not a fix?' I said. 'But not now. Later, maybe. When it's dark.'

'Why when it's dark?' said the Asian.

'I just prefer doing it when it's dark,' I said. 'Why? Is it against the law or something?'

They laughed. Then the skinhead said: 'Where you from anyway, dad? You ain't from round here.'

'I never ask questions like that,' I said. 'In fact, I hardly ever ask questions at all.'

Someone said: 'Yeah. Bad habit.'

'I reckon e's got a job on,' said the Asian boy. 'That right, dad?'

'Well, if I had,' I said, 'I wouldn't go round telling people like you about it.'

'Look at this,' said the Asian boy suddenly. He had a knife in his hand quick as a gust of wind; then with another gust it went *sluck!* into the balk of timber that shored up the burned-out house. I hate knives; I've always hated them—I hate them worse than guns. The Asian boy looked at me to see if he'd got any reaction. But I said: 'I'm off to the pub.'

'Which pub?' said the skin.

'You will keep asking questions,' I said. 'You will keep doing it, won't you?'

'All right, dad.' He was needling me. 'Keep your syrup on.'

I was getting sick of being called dad. 'And don't call me dad,' I said. 'I'm not old enough to be your dad.'

'You look old to me,' said the skinhead.

'Anyone would look old to you.'

'You tryinter ave a go?' said the skinhead incredulously. 'You? At me? You must be bonkers, dad.'

'Ah, drop it, Scar,' said the Asian. I could see he wanted to make his sale.

'What pub again?' one of them said.

'The Agincourt.'

'Then you are bonkers,' said the skinhead called Scar. 'No one but a mad geezer'd go in there. Not at night.'

'Well, I'm going in,' I said.

'Meetin' someone?'

'That's right,' I said. 'Malcolm Muggeridge. He's an old mate.' I turned to the car.

'That's all right, dad,' said the skinhead. 'Listen, don't bother gettin' in, just throw us the keys. No sweat, I don't want to have to hurt you, but it's a nice motor.'

'You want the keys,' I said, 'you'll have to come and get them.'

The Asian boy said: 'Ah, come on, Scar, turn it up.'

'Why don't you shut your black gob?' said the skinhead, and to me: 'Are you giving, dad, or am I coming?'

'Looks like you're coming,' I said, 'you little maniac.'

There were a lot of heads at the windows now, and the street had suddenly gone quiet. The last window was still opening when Scar came in fast with his left hand out flat in front of him; there was a length of bike chain in his right, and he was flailing it. There was something about his eyes that looked wrong as he came in. I blocked the chain with my left forearm; it cut straight through my anorak and marked the skin. I stamped very hard on his right instep. Now you're not going anywhere, I thought, and gave him my head up his nose. I caught the chain as he dropped it and slung it over a roof, feeling where he had filed the links sharp. I stamped on his other foot, cupped my hand under his chin, and threw him at somebody's front door. He went through it. After a while he crawled back out onto the doorstep and started to feel himself all over, trying not to cry with the pain in his feet.

'Anyone else, now?' I said.

Nobody said anything.

'I hate that kind of thing,' I said, turning back to the car,

'especially when I've got a lot on my mind. It gets right
on my wick.'

'E's a bit of a nut, Scar is,' said the Asian boy. 'You don't
want to bother about him too much.'

'I'm not,' I said. The skinhead was trying not to scream
now, while he struggled to get his kickers off his swollen
feet.

'Dad didn't look like e ad it in im,' somebody said.

'They never do,' said the Asian boy. He said to me: 'Tell
you what, maybe I could get you a bird if dark meat don't
bother you.'

'Another time,' I said, getting into the car. 'But I'll tell
you this much, you've got the makings of a businessman,
I reckon.'

'Well, you gotter graft,' he said, leaning in at the
window. 'What about the other deal, then? The smoke.
The fix. You know.'

'You could meet me outside the Agincourt around closing
time if you liked.' I started backing the car out.

'You won't last long in the Agincourt, you bastard!'
screamed the skinhead. 'I'm gointer get you done over in
there!'

'Ah, shut up,' somebody said. 'You're just a nut.'

He still only had one boot off, and his feet stank.

13

Staniland's tape says:

Barbara was hatched in fury like a wasp, and
she'll die in fury. Her promiscuity is aggression; she
uses sex to obliterate a man—this is her revenge
on existence. She forces me to assert myself, then
cuts me down by refusing to have intercourse, and
enslaves me. Every time I succeed in making love to
her she leaves me; she knows this is the worst
punishment she can inflict. Sometimes she varies
the treatment. Last night in the Agincourt, for
instance, she let herself be picked up by the
Laughing Cavalier; she took him back to Romilly
Place with her. Everyone roared with laughter at me
as they left, the two of them. She said I could
come back as well and watch if I liked; the idea
sickened me so much that I went outside and *was*
sick. I spent the whole night walking round London.
There was a north wind blowing; the street lights
looked brilliant in a sudden frost. I was sobered by
the shock of what she had done; even so, I beat
my fists against a wall and cut them. Two
patrolling coppers pushed me up against a fence
by some waste ground at one point, down by

Rotherhithe, but I had money on me and could
prove I wasn't a vagrant, so they let me go after I
had talked to them for a while. They said nothing
at all; their faces were just blank under their
helmets. I don't remember what I said.

I realize I can't satisfy Barbara in bed. I don't
believe anybody can. It's a strange form of love,
to be compelled to convert the woman you love into
a human being. She hates my love, she says; she
says it's servile; she just wants to kick it to pieces.
About a week after what I've just related, we were
in our room one afternoon with the curtains drawn,
and I was feeling over her body. She drew away,
bored, and remarked: 'I've never had an orgasm in
my life, not even when I wank. I don't really
know what I bother to have sex for.'

But I know. She has it out of hatred. Later in the
afternoon I managed to fuck her through her
knickers. She started by pushing me off, as usual;
then suddenly she just shrugged and let me do it.
'You'll have to get me a new pair,' was all she said
when I'd finished. 'Why do you always manage to
make me feel worse afterwards than before?' I asked
her. She lay back on our mattress and lit a
cigarette. 'Look, Charlie,' she said, 'I mean this—
why don't you try and find somebody else?' 'I
don't want anybody but you,' I said. 'Christ,' she
said, 'you just bring out the very worst in me.
You make me really enjoy hating you.' I rolled over
on our mattress away from her and wept. She
took no notice, but went over to the cooker and
made herself a cup of tea, whistling 'Vincent'.

I spent all afternoon in a state of misery and rage.
'I know you're going to ask me for money at some
point,' I said to her. 'You're not much use for
anything else, are you?' she answered.

That evening I was violent with her. It had been
boiling up in me all day, but it began when she
said: 'I'm bored. I'm getting up. I'm going out.'

'Out? Out where?'

'Just out.'

'To the Agincourt?'

'I don't know. Anyway, I shan't need you hanging
around, you're enough to make a monkey weep.
Just give me some money, a tenner'll do.'

'I haven't got much money. I haven't had a
chance to cash a cheque.'

'I'll make some.'

'I wish you wouldn't say things like that. I wish
you wouldn't even talk about going with other
men. I'll tell you what, I'll come with you.'

'I said no.'

All at once my hands were in her hair. I don't
even remember doing it, but I picked up one of
her shoes and hit her on the side of the head with
it. I've never done such a thing to anyone in my
life before. She didn't scream or anything; she just
lay back again on the mattress looking away from
me, with blood running down her face.

'Well,' was all she said. 'Well, well.'

I knew I had lost any ground with her that I'd
ever made.

'Now you won't go anywhere!' I shouted.

'Wrong,' she said. She put the bloody corner of
the sheet to her head, got up, went over to the
sink, dragging the sheet after her, and started cleaning
herself up. She was naked, and her sex looked
huge as she bent over the sink with her back to me.
Her breasts looked awful, too; they always do
when she isn't wearing a bra.

'I want you again,' I groaned in spite of myself.
'It isn't as if I were impotent.'

'You're worse than impotent,' she said into the
mirror above the sink, 'you're a bore, Charlie. I'm
fed up with you; who needs all that intellectual crap
you go in for?'

'I'm sorry I hit you. I truly am.'

'No harm done,' she said, 'except to you.' She
started dressing. 'You spend your life apologizing.
You shouldn't. Never apologize. Never explain.'

'Where are you going?'

'Some club. Maybe an African club. I feel like
some Africans, they're uncomplicated.'

'They're violent, those clubs.'

'I know what they're like,' she said, 'I've been
working them since I was fifteen. Anyway, violence
and pleasure—you can't have one without the other.
You should know.' She added: 'You can stay in all
night if you like; I shan't bring anyone back to this
shithole. I shan't be back till tomorrow sometime
anyway—maybe not till the day after, or the day
after that.'

'Well, take your ten pounds,' I said.

'Fuck the ten pounds,' she said. She went out,
slamming the door. It was a door you had to slam
to shut it properly, but to me it sounded like an
indefinite departure. It always did when she
slammed it. The noise her high heels made on the
staircase sounded final, too.

14

It was nine when I got to the Agincourt, and the place was
full. The man with the face like a snake's was there,
talking to a mild-looking bloke in glasses, but I couldn't see
anyone who looked like the Laughing Cavalier. The
governor wasn't there, either. When I asked the barman
about him, he said he'd had to be hospitalized on account
of his face, which had turned septic.

I ordered a pint of lager—it came up warm again—and
leaned my back on the bar. In a corner not far off sat a
lovely quartet of National Fronters. Two of them were
mods and the third a rocker (normally they were mortal
enemies); he had polished nails studded into his leather
jacket and a Maltese cross round his neck on a silver
chain. Satan sprouted cheerily up out of his collar, too, and
licked at his left ear; I could visualize the patient tattooing
sessions in a cell at Wandsworth. The fourth individual was
studious-looking, about thirty. He wore rimless glasses,
a pretty Fair Isle sweater, and longish blond hair
combed neatly back like intellectual, well-brought-up
boys used to have back in the sixties. He was drinking
a fizzy lemonade, and it was obvious who was in charge
of the meeting.

'Himmler, Heydrich and Goering were responsible for
the exterminations,' studious was saying, 'not the Führer.

74

The Führer was involved with running the war. The Führer just didn't *know* about them.'

'But you just said e was God,' objected one of the mods. 'If e was like God, God always knows what's going on. I know about that, we did a bit of God at school.'

'Next question?' said studious, ignoring him.

'Well, what are we gointer be actually left with,' said the other mod, 'when the National Socialist revolution's all over, like?'

'Just the British,' said studious. 'Pure white Britons.'

'Yeah,' said the rocker, 'well, talking of that, why don't we make a start? I'm bored in here. Why don't we go over to their club across the road and see if we c'n find a golly.'

I tapped him on the shoulder just as he was getting up. 'Just a minute, sonny,' I said. 'I'm joining you for a minute, isn't that nice of me?'

Studious began: 'Nobody—'

I said: 'In 1944 a German soldier took a snap of a little girl of five with her mother and sisters. Sort of family outing, you might say. They'd picked a lovely spot for it, too—walking up the road to the death camp at Treblinka. They'd had their ticket all paid by lovely, kind Hitler; they'd been standing in their own and other people's shit in a cattle-truck, mate, and all in the dark. Wasn't that a lovely holiday for them? And the best thing of all, my old darlings, was that at the end of the day they were told they were just going off for a bath, but that was a blag, see, because they was all gassed. Little girl of five and all.'

There was a short silence. Then the talkative mod tried an unaffected yawn and said: 'Well, we ain't got no kiddies,' and studious sneered: 'You should have been a public speaker, sport.'

'Well, I'm not,' I said, 'I'm a copper, and talking of deaths, I'm investigating a nasty one.' I got out the morgue shot of Staniland and flipped it on the table. But

before anyone could say anything else, a voice behind me
said: 'Might I just look at that?'

I twisted round in my chair and saw a big man, meaty,
around forty, with orange hairs on his forearms, and on
his head. He said to me: 'I'm Harvey Fenton. Did I hear
you say you was fuzz?'

I gave him my warrant card to look at. He said:
'Things've got a bit sad when four lads can't have a quiet
chat in a boozer without you lot butting in.'

'Oh, I don't know,' I said. 'They were lucky I didn't give
them a chance to rabbit on some more—I might have had
the whole lot of them for conspiracy.'

Fenton said: 'It's gettin like South Africa or something
round here.'

'Better than Nazi Germany,' I said. I said to the others:
'You lot can piss off and find another table. Better still,
another pub.' I said to Fenton: 'Sit down, I want to talk to
you.' I flipped the photograph across to him. 'Just have a
look at it, will you? And don't tell me you don't know who he
is, because you do.'

He studied the dreadful picture. 'Know him by sight,' he
said, 'yes. E used to come in here. Pain in the arse. Name
of Stan or something. What happened to him? Looks as if
e'd bin hit with a truck.'

'No, he was beaten to death with a hammer,' I said. 'The
knife went in, too, also the boot.'

'Oh, yes?' said Fenton. 'Sounds like he must've got up
somebody's nose.' He picked his own nose absently.
'Anyway, what makes you think I can help you?'

'Let's say you fit a description.'

He looked straight at me. 'Now don't come the acid,' he
said. He looked down and inspected what he had got out
of his nose on the ball of his thumb.

'Well, I'm just asking questions at this stage,' I said, 'but
we know it's murder. Anyone who thought we were going

to accept it as a hit-and-run was either a half-wit or fucking cheeky.'

'Starsky and Hutch haven't a chance of keeping up with you,' said Fenton. He sniggered.

'One more remark like that,' I said, 'and you're going to make an enemy you don't really need. You've been in the building trade, haven't you?'

'How do you know that?'

'Because I've got a good memory,' I said, 'and now I know your name I know a lot more about you. You've got mates in the scrap-metal and transport business, as well as in clubs. Now I wonder if anyone not three million miles from this pub might have hammered Staniland to death, taken him over to Acton on wheels and dumped him in some bushes there. What do you think?'

'I think askin questions is dangerous,' said Fenton, 'that's what I think.'

'That what I say to myself everytime I write out my resignation,' I said. 'But I always tear the letter up. Did you fuck Staniland's bird, by the way? They say you're a bit of a lad for that.'

'No,' he said. He sighed with hatred.

'I'm not all that surprised,' I said. 'For my money, you're just an old pouf at heart.'

Fenton clenched his fists on the table until the knuckles turned white. 'By Christ,' he said, 'it's a bloody lucky thing for you you are a copper, because if you hadn't of been, you might of been in a fair way to get yourself badly hurt.'

'You can cut that out, dear,' I said. 'With your form they'd weigh you off for seven if you squashed a fly.'

'We haven't met before, have we?'

'We don't need to have. Not with the file you've got. Every copper knows it by heart.'

He thought about that, then called across to the barman: 'Hey, top em up, Joe. On me.' The barman was busy serving, but he dropped everything to rush over with Fenton's round. 'Good boy!' said Fenton. 'Good lad. Fine!' He lifted his whisky. 'Cheers!' he said to me, grinning.

'Let's get into what you really had against Staniland,' I said.

'Nothing! He was just a drag.'

'You just took the piss out of him, is that it? You sure you didn't screw his bird?'

'Why should I bother? I've got my own birds. Anyway, if I had of screwed her, what difference would it of made?'

'Things might have got hairy,' I said. 'I'm really looking to see if you're not tied into this thing. Didn't you beat him up once? Out behind the gents there?'

'No I didn't!'

'Little bits and pieces of things I've heard tell me you're lying.'

'Little bit and pieces of things add up to fuck all,' he said, 'specially in court.'

'You should know,' I said, 'you've had plenty of practice in there.'

'Well, I can't tell you anything at all.'

'Okay, then I'll tell you what,' I said, 'how'd you like to come over to the Factory with me now and tell Chief Inspector Bowman all the things you won't tell me? You'd get a sympathetic hearing from Bowman, you would—he absolutely loves individuals like you.'

'I'm not mad about Poland Street,' he said, 'to be honest. They're a bit too keen on custom-built engineering over there.'

'Well, you'd better try harder answering some questions in that case,' I said. 'Here's one—do you know where the governor of this pub is? Fat bloke. Got his face hurt.'

'Seems he's gone,' said Fenton. 'Seems they don't think he'll be back.'

'Septic lip?'

'That's one way of putting it,' Fenton said. 'But I heard someone told him e chattered too much and to button it. But he couldn't find his needle, too bad.'

'Sounds like one for Lewisham to me,' I said. 'Could be "grievous bodily harm." '

'Now look,' he said. 'You're really into me, aren't you?' He took a long pull at his double Scotch, but he was calm. Yes, I thought, you're a dangerous bastard. 'You're not going to give me a john over that cunt's face, are you?'

'Well, I don't know,' I said. 'But if you do find there's a warrant out for you, it could be because you wouldn't cooperate with me over this Staniland business.'

'I keep telling you, he was just a pain, that's all.'

'So you never beat him up. Never screwed his bird. Just stood right back and took the mickey, but you never touched him. You were almost like mates.'

'That's right.'

'The governor here might crack and say the opposite, if he felt safe enough.'

'I don't think so,' said Fenton. 'Down to being into the river like he was, I believe he's by way of having a breakdown right now. Unreliable witness—the Public Prosecutors couldn't do anything with him.'

'The more you go on talking,' I said, 'the more you go on lying. It's funny with you. Now I'm convinced that Staniland died not half a square mile from here. Yet he was found right the way over in Acton.'

'I don't know west London at all,' said Fenton. He yawned.

'Well, if you don't, the A to Z street guide does. That's no problem.'

'Look,' shouted Fenton, 'I've ad about enough. You're trying to fit me up for this, aren't you?'

'I'm trying to find out who killed him,' I said, 'and I've got a funny idea I'm not doing badly at all.'

'Why pick on me? All I can tell you is that some of the

lads in here—all right, I was one of them—asked this
bloke quite nicely if he wouldn't mind patronizing some
other establishment. He said no, he liked it here, and kept
coming back legless, sometimes with that brass of his, and
kept bending everybody's ear off. And that's all I know.'

'People ever call you the Laughing Cavalier?' I said.

'The what? No, never.'

'Funny, I can just see why people might, sometimes.' I lit
a Palace filter. It tasted revolting; I only smoke them
because I hope they might help me give it up. 'All right,' I
said, 'we could go on like this all night, but we won't—I
shan't come back for you till I've got a case.'

'If you can get one. I keep telling you, none of this is
down to me.'

'Well, if I run out of folks to fit the hat, Harvey,' I said,
'who knows, you might just have to do. After all, I
wouldn't need a watertight case, not with the form you've
got—it's as long as that arm of yours with the orange hairs
on it.'

He didn't say anything, he just looked at me. He had
started to look worried, and no wonder. I added: 'Do you
and your mates go in for torture, by the way?'

'Christ, no!' he shouted. 'What do you think we are?
Animals?'

'You bet that's what I think,' I said. 'After all, there was
Williamson, you remember, the supergrass; you smashed
both his legs with an iron bar and dumped him on the M20.
Ten years' preventive detention you drew for that, I
recall, only they paroled you after seven, what for I can't
think.'

'Look, that was different,' said Fenton anxiously. 'That
time, I admit, it was squarely down to me—the ice cream
grassed me over that Whitgift Street bank job.'

'Well, I still think you're mixed up in this Staniland case,'
I said.

'You'll have a job proving it.'

'You short of money, Harvey?' I said. It was a question
that fazed people like Harvey. If he said he wasn't, I
might start digging into where he'd got it. If he said he was,
I might try to find out what ideas he had about filling the
gap. In the end he said: 'Who isn't short of it?'

'A few hundred would always come in handy, wouldn't
it?'

'Staniland was broke.'

'No, he wasn't. Not till right at the end, anyway.'

'How do you know?'

'All I'll tell you is this,' I said. 'Staniland did a lot of
writing, did you know?'

'No, I didn't. I didn't know anything about him, I tell
you.'

'And I mean a lot of writing,' I said. 'And he recorded a
lot on cassettes, too. And guess who's got it all? That's
right—I have, over at the Factory.'

He turned white. 'You find my name on any of it?'

'There's a description that could fit you. Like the orange
hairs on your arms.' I gazed at them pointedly.

'That won't get you far,' said Fenton. 'Thousands of men
have orange hair on their arms. And anyway, one middle-
aged drunken nut droning away on a cassette don't add up
to anything much.'

'Even so,' I said, 'don't fly off to Morocco for any
sunshine without letting me know.' I scribbled the number
of the Factory down and passed it to him. 'Okay, on your
bike. You're still clean until I can prove you aren't.' We
got up. 'I've enjoyed our little talk.'

'Likewise,' he said, moving away, 'I don't think.'

When I got out into the street I saw someone standing by
my car.

'Well,' I said. 'If it isn't the businessman.'

'You still want in on our deal?' said the Asian boy.

'Sure,' I said. 'Let's get round to Romilly Place.'

When we arrived he was out of the car and up over the

street wall. He whispered from the top: 'Wait there.' I got out of the car, but I didn't hear anything until the street door of number seven squeaked open.

'Okay, come in,' he breathed. He shut us inside, then bolted the door. 'The light's bin cut off.'

'Doesn't matter,' I said, 'I've got a flashlight.' I shone it on the filthy stairs.

'I've got the gear,' he said.

'Another time,' I said, 'I've changed my mind.' I gave him a twenty-pound note.

He examined it in the torchlight. 'Paying me to get lost, are you?'

'You should care.'

'You know something?' he said. 'I believe you're a copper.' When I didn't say anything he said: 'You gointer bust me?'

'Lucky for you I've got other things on my mind,' I said. 'But you want to be careful how you push smack to strangers, otherwise you won't be on the street much longer.'

'Maybe I could bust you,' he whispered thoughtfully.

'Don't let your amazing brilliance go to your head,' I said. 'Coppers stick to each other like shit to a blanket, you can't win, you ought to know that by now.'

'Anyway, fancy taking money off a copper. Usually it's the other way round, you bribe them.'

'Don't let's go into principles,' I said. 'Just take the twenty and fuck off. It's like any other money, it spends.'

'Okay,' he said, 'see you.'

As soon as he had gone I looked round the rooms on the ground floor. There were three of them. It looked as if the landlord had had his quarters down here. There were all the signs that he and whoever he had lived with had left in a hurry. Torn paper and old rent books were spread all over the floor, there was a stripped bedstead with one leg jacked up on a brick; a urine stain in the centre of the mattress curled importantly in the material like the dirty oval frame of an old picture; a stock of horror comics had toppled over in a corner. The room opposite was the same except that the wallpaper was peeling off and it stank worse because the bucket that had been used to piss in hadn't been emptied. 'Christ,' I muttered, 'who'd be a copper?' The back room had been converted into a bathroom and toilet; a rat slid up the wall as I opened the door, with a flick of its fat tail. I was surprised no squatters had moved in; maybe the news hadn't had a chance to do the rounds yet.

I went up the stairs quickly, but trod on the side next the wall to stop them creaking—there might just still be guests. I needn't have worried: nothing followed me up the stairwell but a smell of garbage. The second door I came to, I sent in and shone the torch round. I was sure it was Staniland's room; any copper can tell where the law's been, they turn everything over twice. All the same I went over it again. Bowman's men were always in a hurry; they had too much work on their hands.

I went to the window to open it and get some air, but it was nailed shut, so I stood in the middle of the bare linoleum floor and wondered what it must have been like, Staniland and Barbara living there together—when she was home. *Home!* There was the cookette in the corner by the window, just as he had described it; there, too, was the sink with the cracked mirror over it where she had fixed her face nonchalantly after he had hit her with the shoe. There was the bedding on the floor where he had muttered his passion for her, and where she had lain back, flicking through the pages of *Playgirl*, while he drunkenly tried to force her thighs apart. I don't believe in ghosts, but that room was thick with death, jostling me in the half dark; the dead man seemed to groan after me to avenge him. This room was in an appalling state, too. The weather was dry at the moment, otherwise I bet it rained in. Large parts of

the ceiling plaster had long ago dropped off in the damp,
exposing the laths; doubtless any lead there had been on
the roof had been ripped off, and probably half the tiles too.

There was a cupboard in the corner next to the mattress;
when I tried it, I found it was still locked. I kicked it open.
There were a few clothes inside, mostly women's, and some
dirty shirts and underwear on the floor. I found nothing
in any of the pockets except a 2p piece; above the clothes-
rail in the cupboard, though, was a shelf with six cassettes
lying at the back, with the names of hard rock groups on
them. I took those.

I searched the place again, but found nothing more.

I left, hoping the council would tear down the whole of
Romilly Place one day, when they stopped screaming
politics at each other and got on with the job the ratepayers
had voted them in for.

15

'Your name Spark? Arthur Spark?'

'That's me, mate,' said the man indifferently, not looking up from his plate.

'I want to talk to you.'

'What for? I don't know you from my tenth pube.'

I showed him my warrant card and discreetly, so that no one at the other tables could see it. That made him put his knife and fork down. 'Oh, Christ, yeah. Yeah, okay, but c'n I get on with my nosh? I'm on shift at two.'

'Eat.'

'All right,' he said, 'what's it down to? I just drive a truck for a living, I aven't done nothing.'

'No one's saying you have. You were married to a woman, maiden name Barbara Ethel Smith?'

'So what if I was? We're divorced.'

'Long time?'

'Must be goin on five year.'

'Any kids?'

'What? With her?' He laughed bitterly. 'You must be joking. All the time we was together she was on the pill.'

'When was the last time you saw her?'

He turned obstinate. 'Don't know. Can't remember.'

'Look,' I said, 'you're not in any shtuck, so why look for bother by withholding information?'

He thought about that. 'If she's in bother, I don't want to say anything that'll get her in deeper.'

'Nobody's saying she's in bother,' I said. 'All I'm trying to do is trace her and ask her some questions. I had my work cut out tracing you.'

'What do you want to question her about?'

I leaned closer towards him across the table. We were in a transport cafe not far from the Hole in the Wall by Waterloo Station. It was bright in there, dinner hour, a fine day; the Formica tables were packed with lorry-drivers eating the meat, mash and two veg, washed down with a pot of tea. He bit into a slice of Wonderloaf with marge on it.

'She'd got mixed up with a bloke who wound up dead in some shrubbery over in West Five last Friday. Very dead.'

'Murder?'

'That's right.'

'I wouldn't have thought Babsie'd've done that,' said Spark. 'She never lost her cool. She had too much bleedin cool if you arst me. Cool. She was fucking freezing, mate.'

'Still, she was mixed up with this man; you can see why I want to talk to her, can't you?' I showed him Staniland's picture. When he had recovered from it, he thought some more. 'Well, I don't know where she lives, squire, if that's what you mean. But I've heard she does the clubs this side of the river. Old Kent Road, the Elephant, you know.'

'Where've you heard that from?'

'Some of my mates have seen her in them, ones that used to know us when we was together. I've remarried, got two little kiddies, so I've no money to throw round in them places, never mind the punch-ups. I can handle myself all right, but it's when they get the knives and shivs out and you find you've got half your face missing.'

'Any particular club?'

He sighed. 'You people do go on and on, don't you?'

'That's what we draw the ratepayers' money for.'

'You tried a pub called the Agincourt, down Greenwich way?'

'Yes.'

'Not very helpful in there, are they?'

'They would have been if I'd leaned on them harder,' I said, 'only I'm not all that keen on throwing my weight about, it's the quickest way of shutting them up.'

That got him more on my side. 'She used to be over at the Hard Rock Club, down by Surrey Docks,' he said at last, 'but that was a while back. Still, you might try it. It's rough in there, but they, like, do a bird for a geezer, see? Mind, as I say, I never see her. The wife wouldn't stand for it, that's only natural, ain't it?' He looked at the clock. 'Christ, I only got fifteen minutes, then I gotter go. You can't take a chance with a job these days—not with three million folks on the dole.'

'This won't take long,' I said. 'Did your ex work the clubs while you were married to her?'

He nodded. 'She bin on em since she was a kid. But it wasn't that I minded so much—what drove me mad was the way she had blokes back at the house, bold as fucking brass, while I was out at work. Any number of em, right under the neighbours' noses. Christ, I even caught er at it one time. I didn't half give er a whack, but it didn't do no good, and I'm not one for thumpin women anyway. Talking of clubs,' he added, 'we met at one. She was a real knockout at eighteen, Babsie was, I can tell you—she'd got style. We started goin together, but I never could really make sense of her. She was a Banana girl—didn't ave no mum or dad. She was like a one-off. Got all her marbles an that, I'm not sayin she adn't, but you could just never get right through to her. Like if you arst er where your dinner was, she'd stare through you like she adn't really heard you, that sort of thing. Unnerved me, it did.'

'Go on.'

'Well, anyway, one day I arst er would she. Would she marry me, I mean. Christ, she went bleedin potty. You can stuff your bleedin marriage, she said, I don't want no kids nor a mortgage or any of that crap. But we'll ave a good fuck (scuse me) if you like—I can't think why you never arst me before, she said. Well, you could've knocked me flat. I'm a man that likes a charver if ever there was one, but my life, that put me right off—I couldn't've got it up that time, not if she'd bin Clordia Cardinal. Still, come to a rub, we did get married, and what a bleedin carve-up, as I say. I was on the buses in them days, the 137 route out of Clapham there. It got to be a nightmare with me, that job; once I knew she was carryin on with other fellers I started nearly missing stops wonderin what the hell was goin on at home an that—I ad to pack it in at the death. I said to myself, this as got to stop, Arthur, otherwise you are gointer go fuckin barmy. So one night I just faced er with it, it was a Sunday, and you know what she said? Okay, okay, she said, keep your syrup on, I can't think why you hung on this long. Well, I said to er, you really are just scum, Babsie, ain't you? Ah, cut it out, she says, and with that she packs just one case of clothes an says you can keep all the rest of the gear, cunt, be seein you. It was hell the first few weeks she was gone; but then suddenly I woke up one morning feelin better, I don't know why. So I got out of bed (I'd bin spending a lot of time in the pit, mopin), ad a wash an shave, went down to the local depot of National Carriers, an got this job. I'd rather bore up the M1 with the radio on anyhow than grind round central London all day in a bus. Mind, I'm not sayin London Transport weren't good employers, look after their people an such, but you get too many fights on the buses now, specially at night. Anyway, come to a rub, I never looked back; I met my wife an we've got the two lovely kiddies an a house out Plumstead way. I just hear about Babsie from my mates now an then, like I said—but I never seen er again, not from that day to this, an that's all I c'n tell you.'

16

'I'm sorry to trouble you like this, Mr. Viner, and thank
you for asking me to lunch. It wasn't necessary.'

'Oh, it's no trouble, and it's quite unusual, having lunch
with a police officer. Let's sit down and have some. It'll
be pretty vile, I'm afraid.'

'Our own canteen's nothing to write home about,' I said.

We were in the BBC cafeteria out at Wood Green. The
surrounding tables were occupied by perennially young
men. Some of them were producers, while others just looked
exactly like producers. There were some pretty girls
sitting around as well who looked as if they, too, fitted into
the organization in some suitably vague way. Anyway,
everyone looked very, very secure in his talent. Viner came
back with our lunches on a tray and doubtfully tackled his
main course, corned beef and gherkins. When I brought up
the subject of Staniland he said: 'I've always had a very
soft spot for Charles. He isn't in any trouble, I hope?'

'Not anymore,' I said. 'I'm afraid he was beaten to death
last Friday.'

'Oh, God,' he said, his mouth dropping open. 'Why?'

'That's what I've got to find out. And who.'

'Why come to me, though? I haven't seen Charles for two
years.'

'I've come to you because he wrote about you. We found

a lot of his writing and some cassettes he'd recorded. I'm
following up every name in them; it's all I've got to go on. I
just want to talk to anyone who knew him; I'm trying to
get any kind of line on him I can.'

'Yes,' said Viner, 'yes, of course. I understand.' He was
only about thirty, but I liked him. He looked as if he had
brains.

'According to Staniland,' I said, 'the BBC took him on as
a scriptwriter. Why at forty-eight? Seems a bit old.'

'He'd submitted a play for television,' Viner said. 'They
didn't do it, of course, it was far too good.'

'I'm sorry, I don't understand.'

'You wouldn't unless you worked here,' said Viner. 'It
did what good work usually does—it hit out too hard. It
was set in South London, which fascinated him, The play
was about tarts, blacks, clubs, drugs and riots; it also
blasted the trendies. It was called 'A Nasty Story,' a title
he'd borrowed from Dostoevsky. I was asked to read it,
and I was the only person who told them, look, you've got
to do it. Of course they wouldn't. Still, they liked his
dialogue enough to give him a trial as an assistant scriptwriter,
and he ended up working with me on serials. I liked him a
lot. He could be bloody funny—and did he have talent! For
writing? Really masses! He could take a ten-page scene,
reduce it to fifty lines of dialogue, and the whole meaning
sprang out at you.' He hesitated. 'When he was on form,
that is.'

'Oh, yes?'

'Well, he drank,' said Viner, 'and I mean he really drank.
The Beeb's idea of drinking in the office is an occasional
pale ale—Charles's was a bottle of Scotch a day. Or two.
Mind, he never passed out; his eyes just used to turn
inward. I remember he was sick into his handkerchief once,
but he was never incoherent, even. The bottle would be
on his desk out in the open, and if a passing bigwig didn't
like it—well, Charles had rather a sharp tongue.'

'Even so,' I said, 'he struck me as pretty vulnerable.'

'Well, yes, he had a skin fewer than most of us. The two things that really reduced him to pulp were boredom and his relations with women.'

'He certainly didn't have much luck with them.'

'Oh, I don't know,' said Viner. 'His wife Margo was all right. Attractive, too. She used to come out here and pick him up sometimes.'

'The name Barbara Spark mean anything to you?'

'I'm afraid not. Who is she?'

'A woman he knew that I'd like to have a word with. Anyway, never mind, go on.'

'Well, after a time, Charles started to get more and more restless here. I can quite understand why, of course—he wanted to write his own stuff, the work he was doing for us showed him his own talent. But there's no room for that kind of thing at Auntie's. Instead—I don't know if you've watched any of a frightful historical series that's just been repeated?'

'Yes, I got an eyeful of it on the box the other night. It was about some king.'

'That's right, the private life of Edward the Confessor. Charles nicknamed it The Pincushion People because the clothes were so ridiculous. He and I had to write the script for it, and it's been repeated. God knows why—its ratings are awful. Anyway, one day Charles said to me: "I just can't stand these ghastly Pincushion scripts we're doing anymore; they're even more depressing than that comedy we tackled, 'Billy Ballpoint'. " "There's nothing we can do about it now," I said. "Oh, don't be so feeble," he said. "Here, pass me that story line." "It's too late to rewrite all that," I shouted at him, "it's been approved, everyone'll have a fit." "All the better reason for rewriting it totally," he said. Next day he had finished one episode. "Here, read it," he said. Christ, I've never laughed so much in my life. Poor old Edward the Confessor, who after all had never been strong on laughs, had been turned totally inside out. One abrupt twist, and he'd turned the whole thing into a farce. "You may be mad," I said when I had finished it, "but you're completely wasted in here—you should be writing gags for a top-line comedian, you'd make a fortune. But it'll never do," I added, throwing it back at him, "they'd crucify you upstairs." "They'll do that anyway sooner or later," he said, "so they might as well get on with it." Whereupon he took it upstairs and slung it in somebody's in-tray. Well, nothing happens in a hurry here, as you probably know; everything's decided by committees all terrified of doing the wrong thing. However, they sent for him a while later, and down he came, duly crucified, and looking cheerful. "Well, they've done it to me," he laughed, rubbing his hands. "I'm fired, thank God. It was worth it, too—that ghastly trendy-leftie producer burst into tears when I told him what I thought of the approved script." "But what are you going to do now?" I said. "Get pissed on my severance cheque," he said. ' "You're not busy, so ring for a cab and let's go up to the Dead Piano Club in Ken Church Street." '

Viner sighed. 'I don't remember much about the next couple of days.'

'And was that the last time you saw him?'

'Yes, I saw what was left of him onto a twenty-two bus at the bottom of Greek Street. I missed him at the Beeb.' He paused. 'Besides, he helped me out once. I got into a bit of shtuck at the bank; couldn't find the money for the rates. Charles fixed me up—three hundred quid. He was like that—do anything for anyone if he could, even for people who sent him up or downright disliked him. "Don't bother paying it back," he said, "you'll do me a favour one of these days." I never did, of course. Do you want the castle pudding with treacle or the ice cream?'

'I'll have the ice cream.'

'Very sensible,' said Viner. 'I do hope to Christ you catch whoever did it.'

'I don't think I'll have much trouble identifying them,' I said. 'It's proving it, that's the snag. They don't like tapes in a court of law—a good barrister can knock that kind of stuff to pieces. Besides, I'm on this alone. It isn't as if we were after the Yorkshire Ripper.'

'I just can't understand how he could have got up anybody's nose to the extent that they'd beat him to death like that,' said Viner. Suddenly he was nearly in tears. He pulled himself together and said: 'I suppose it must have been some kind of nut?'

'Yes, probably. I don't want them to get out of it that way, though.'

'Whatever else was the matter with Charles,' said Viner, 'he was a lovely man.' He put a lump of sugar into his powdered coffee and stirred it. The liquid swirled darkly as the sugar went down. He drank up his coffee quickly and looked at the wall clock. The lunch hour was over; the canteen had grown quiet and empty. We were both silent; there was nothing more to say. After a moment Viner whispered: 'I must go now.' He shook hands with me and hurried away.

17

I put on another of Staniland's tapes:

Most people live with their eyes shut, but I mean
to die with mine open. We all instinctively try to
make death less difficult for ourselves. Personally,
I've got two ways. First, I drink. I drink for
oblivion, and then a fall of some kind or a blow,
once I'm beyond thinking and feeling. That's how
I'd die, with my eyes shut. My other way is to
rationalize my experience. But, no matter now
logically you think, you soon get in a muddle.
Existence is blind—neither for you nor against you.
This impartiality contradicts everything in human
experience; there is neither love nor hatred, caresses
or assault, in your dealing with the everyday.
Existence is like a stock exchange—you can make as
big a fool of yourself as you like, and go on until
you're hammered. Look at Duéjouls. What a gruelling
experience that was. To buy that great ruined
house in the middle of nowhere, with the last of
that money from my brother, and then pray like
Micawber for something to turn up, so that I could
renovate the place and turn it into something. I
couldn't get anywhere with what I wrote; Margo

always said I never would. She said flatly that I
was too old, too out-of-date and too drunk. We used
to have the most frightful quarrels about it in the
kitchen at Duéjouls, while the rain leaked through
the rafters with the regular beat of a clock. Yet it
was all right while she and Charlotte were there.
She always cheered me up, always said: 'It'll be
all right, Daddy,' coming in from school and
throwing her books on the settle, then going up to
her room to listen to John Travolta.

But afterwards. When they'd gone. Loneliness
distorts you in the countryside.

Nothing turned up. No money came. I was at the
end of my resources. I was thrown back onto
prising tomorrow's money out of the day after. For
five years I was a peasant, and switched my brain
off. I cut timber on the *causses* with a chainsaw in
the winter. The snow was blue up there against
the grey air; at eight hundred metres the clouds
came right down on your back among the oak
thickets. In the summer I took a *harpe* and went
from one vineyard to another in the great heat,
wherever I could get work from the peasants. I look
at myself in the mirror here, now, in London, and
marvel how I ever could have done it. *Déchausser:*
cutting the weeds away from the root of each
vine. Two thousand vines—always uphill—a gulp of
wine after the next row (eighty metres to a row);
no, the next, I can hang on—I must hang on. I
worked alone and singing to keep the solitude at
bay in the gusting heat and the wind that sweeps up
the valley, boiling you to your naked waist. They
won't get me out of here, I kept saying to myself;
whatever else collapses around you, it won't be
you. I was too old for the work; the young men
who worked with me kept telling me I was too

old. But I kept going—seven in the morning until
seven at night with an hour off at midday. I
became as hard as whipcord, but with a brain like
cottonwool. I just coasted vaguely over the past.
To bed exhausted at night, with the alarm clock set
for six in the morning, and the next, and the next.
A bath occasionally, and my aching legs relaxed
against the clean rough sheet. I had no need to
think—and not a fuck in all that time, not even with
Margo: just the utter quiet at night except for the
stream below, panting like an old locomotive in a
station. I can do it, I said to myself, even if I'm
too old really. My hands bled at first, and I was
slow. But I was stolid and painstaking and oh,
God, I needed the money for us to eat with, the
three of us, and the minimum wage was only
seventy-eight francs a day when I started.

The house had sixteen rooms. After Margo and
Charlotte had gone, I would talk to myself out
loud all day in the kitchen where I had moved my
bed and my gear; the other fifteen were empty
(now that I had burned all their clothes), except for
the bats. I did the roof in my spare time, so that
it didn't leak anymore.

I didn't ask my brother for anything—at least, not
until I got back to Britain. And even then I only
dropped a hint or two. Working on the land down
at Duéjouls had made me proud. But when I saw
I wouldn't get anything from him and my sister-in-
law, I went on the dole for a while over the river
there in Battersea, where I had found lodgings. All
I had left were a thousand pounds' worth of
equities which I'd intended for Charlotte, but I was
hungry. I cheated; I didn't declare the equities to
the Department of Health and Social Security
Papers. Why the fucking hell should I? I was

nearly fifty, and I'd never claimed anything from
the state before in my life—it had all been the
other way round. Still, it was interesting, being
interviewed at the DHSS. The black man behind
the counter asked me if I was really British. I slid
my passport across without a word, but I was
thinking: I'm a fucking sight more British than you
are, at any rate. However, I didn't say anything
in case he wrote 'Refused' across my application. I
couldn't afford to have that happen because I was
broke by then, having had to give my stepson Eric
some money, and I needed something for rent and
food. I needed a drink, too, but I wasn't in France
anymore with wine at two francs a litre—here it
was two pounds. This was when I wrote that play
for the BBC and got a job there. In the play,
which I called 'A Nasty Story', a title I borrowed
from the Russian (you can keep Tolstoy), I asked
what you were supposed to do in London with the
tenner a week that's left over from your supplementary
benefits once you've paid the rent. I had nothing
left for me in France; I'd made the house over to
Charlotte with a local *notaire* in case something
happened to me. As for my rent in Battersea, I
had to pay it on the dot as soon as I'd collected my
Girocheque, otherwise I'd have been locked out with all
my gear inside. It happened to a few people in that house.
The landlord just waited his chance—what a bastard! He
must have made a small fortune like that: all it cost him was
changing the lock.

It was after I'd gone out one night and got pissed
instead of paying the rent that I went to work for
Planet. I saw their ad in the evening paper while I
was sitting in the Princess Caroline in Battersea
Park Road. Planet didn't ask questions—just did
you have a current driver's license, and it was

cash. Instead of asking questions, they worked the
shit out of you, the Creamleys did. Forty a week
rent for the clapped-out old motor they hired you,
another forty a week to the office for the business—
you pay your repairs, you pay the petrol, you pay
the insurance, you pay every fucking thing.
Anything you had left over was your own. That
wasn't much. The ad promised you could make a
hundred and fifty a week—they just forgot to say
that it was gross. I couldn't take more than a
hundred and fifty gross in a good week anyhow.
Once the recession started, you'd got two cars to
half a punter. The Creamleys didn't care if there
were drivers queuing for a job all the way down
the stairs—they were taking forty a week off each of
them, weren't they? Whether they got any work
or not. The ones that didn't like it could piss off;
there were plenty more unemployed drivers.

I might have forty a week to live on if I was dead
lucky, say, one week in four, if I didn't get
clobbered for my drops. Unlucky, I'd have to try
and get a sub from Creamley: 'What's the matter,
Two Four? You broke again? Here, here's twenty,
have a drink on me.' It was all right for drivers
with capital—they'd invested it in Rollers or Mercs,
and got all the airport and wedding jobs, also
taking Pakistani businessmen up to their factories in
the north. But what could you expect to get with
a clapped-out rented Maxi? No, you don't get the
meaty jobs with a '74 Maxi, not with the upholstery
burst on the back seat.

Financial disaster could strike you easily on my
margin. I remember the night—I knew I had rust
in the wheel arches—when the rear suspension
collapsed when I was POB to Dollis Hill with
three Turkish waiters from the Ef-Es Kebab on

board. They were good about it—said it was only
a ten-minute walk to their place now anyway. They
even tried to give me the money for the fare. I
wouldn't take it, though, because they'd been good
about the breakdown and because I hadn't got
them home. Well, it was three in the morning when
they left with newspapers over their heads, it was
pissing with rain, the way it only seems to in North
London—really cold, really hard, really wet. I
had to phone a garage to tow me in. Creamley said:
'Christ, you again, Two Four.' I had to pay for a
new back axle, two weeks' wages. It was throwing
money away on that wreck. Creamley said: 'You
gotter understand, Two Four—if I started paying
my drivers' repairs, where'd my profit be, mate?'
And he had to lecture me. He said: 'The trouble with
you is, Charlie, you don't work long enough hours.
You can't hope to make cabbing pay if you don't sweat
at it.' I said: 'I am sweating at it; I got a private
life too, though.' 'So've I,' he said 'only I keep it where
it belongs.' 'Where's that?' 'In bed,' he says, 'or else
doing the books—it's common sense, Two Four.'

Some of the punters, when you did get them,
were no good, either. Not like the Turks. After
the Jewish businesswomen, the worst of the lot
were the Africans and the Japanese, in my
experience. 'Don't you know your fuckin way,
man? You white, an you don't know your own
city?' 'Don't you know the short cut to Camden
Square, driver?' 'I don't like this nasty old car, it
smells. Stop, driver. Radio for another.'

The tough drivers just used to tell them to
fucking well get out and walk. . . .

I rewound Staniland's tape and put it with the pile on the
kitchen table, whose Formica glittered back at me blue

under the central light. Then I opened a cold can of
export beer and tried to think back to the castle that
Staniland's sister-in-law had said they had once had, and
from there through the tortured points in the course of his
life that had led him to cabbing a rusty old Maxi five
nights a week for Planet, and from that to this Spark
woman, and from that to the terrible way he had died—
in agony, and then contemptuously kicked and dragged by
his killers into that wet shrubbery in Albatross Road.
Where I identified with Staniland, what I had inherited
from him, was the question why.

Mind, I had always asked it myself—but this why was
not a copper's why. Staniland's question was the question
I had once read on a country gravestone erected to a child
of six: 'Since I was so early done for, I wonder what I
was begun for.'

Though Staniland had died at the age of fifty-one, he
still had the innocence of a child of six. The naïve
courage, too—the desire to understand everything, whatever
the cost.

This fragile sweetness at the core of people—if we
allowed that to be kicked, smashed and splintered, then
we had no society at all of the kind I felt I had to uphold. I
had committed my own sins against it, out of transient
weakness.

But I hadn't deliberately murdered it for its pitiful
membrane of a little borrowed money, its short-lived
protective shell—and that was why, as I drank some more
beer and picked up the next of Staniland's tapes, I knew I
had to nail the killers.

Not just know them. Nail them. I switched on the
player:

On the terrace at Duéjouls, sixty feet above the
road. Boiling hot, sitting in a wicker chair. A great
butterfly, the biggest I've ever seen, lands in front

of me. It's black, gold and purple; it must be nearly
ten centimetres across. Its wings shuffle in the
roaring south wind which will bring rain in two
days. The butterfly clings to the sunlit stones
with difficulty; then it's whirled away over the roof,
its flight mindless yet circumstantial, like the
pleasure of singing. A lizard darts from under the
vine that shades me. It is primitive, yet an exact
purpose in itself. Its tongue flickers; it stares sideways,
poised for food or flight. It gasps with excitement
under its scaly skin—it runs towards me unafraid,
its existence elsewhere as long as I don't move.
But I cough over my cigarette and its head shoots
up, the eyes and tongue flutter in a blur of
movement—it is gone.

Physically I am here in Lewisham, but I am
remembering the time when I worked at the hotel
in Duéjouls. It is early January, half-past six in the
morning, and the thermometer when I got on my
Mobylette to go down to work said minus twelve.
Behind the hotel, which is shut up for the winter,
four of us are assembled to kill a pig. There is one
dim light in the sty, and eight uneasy pigs.

'Not that one,' says the *patron*, Jean, 'she's on
heat. Any of the others yes, that one, fine, the
male.'

We surround and grab it; I get the rope with the
noose round its hind legs and pull it tight. The
pig is squealing; it knows all right.

'Makes you feel like a criminal, doesn't it?' says
Loulou, one of the men. He is squat, dark and
young, with a broken nose. I work for him
sometimes, and he reminds me of an engraving I
once saw of Napoleon after the incident at Toulon
early in his career. I agree with him. I feel like an
executioner, too. It's to do with the atmosphere in

the sty—the dark, the single dim bulb, the intense,
still cold. The only thing missing is the shot of
cognac to give the victim before we do it to him.

'Up on the bale with him,' says Jean, pulling the
other rope tight on the animal's forelegs.

It takes all of us; the pig weighs a hundred and
ninety kilos. Loulou and I hold the back legs I
have lassoed; the others hold it by its front legs, and
it writhes frantically on the straw. Somebody tugs
on its ears, dragging the head back to expose its
throat to the knife. Shut off in the next sty, over a
low brick wall, the other pigs shuffle around grunting
with fear, infected by the approaching death in
their midst. Ours snarls and squeals. If only it were
stupid! But nothing is.

'Quickly, now,' Jean says to the slaughterer.

I can smell death mixed with the smell of pigshit;
it is a sharp, pungent smell, but not clean. The
slaughterer aproaches slowly in his rubber apron, a
sixty-five-year-old peasant with rheumatism,
sharpening a long knife on a steel sharpener.

'Now then!' says Jean sharply.

In goes the knife, a single thrust, point first, low
into the right side of the throat down by the
collarbone; the blood instantly starts to whistle out
into the casserole that the slaughterer's wife is
holding against the wound. They want to catch the
blood to make black pudding with—a little garlic
and mixed herbs with it, a *sanquette*, delicious. At
first the pig screams louder than ever. The blood
spurts out, a deep scarlet with bubbles in it; it
steams in the cold, heavy air. Now the pig shits
over my legs in its throes, then pisses into the straw
bale. Loulou next to me gets a kick on the elbow
and shouts: '*Ah, putain de merde!*' The blood spatters
feverishly, irregularly now, into the tin pot; now

the animal's struggles weaken. Still, it takes it ten
minutes to die, and even then—

'You can leave go now.'

I come round and look into the pig's eyes where it
lies on its side. Its big body is bloodless, has gone
white. Dying, its jaws are half open and it shows its
yellow teeth; it looks up and beyond me with an
expression of disgust.

'It's still alive.'

'No, no, it's dead, Charles.' The slaughterer's
wife has already started cutting into its snout;
they've got another one to do before lunch.

But I was sure it wasn't dead.

'That's just its nerves,' said the slaughterer. 'All
right, let's get it onto the big ladder and carry it
out. Easy, now.'

'Couldn't you electrocute it?' I said, when we had
got outside. The sun was coming up at last,
glaring yellow through the naked branches in the
hotel garden.

'Of course not,' said the slaughterer. 'You've got
to get all the blood out. As long as the heart's
beating, that acts as a pump, that's what gets all the
blood out, see? The animal's working for you like
that.'

I said to Loulou quietly: 'That was awful.' I
didn't feel faint or sick, just cold inside.

'Yes,' said Loulou, 'well, but what's the use? If
you don't kill the fucking thing, you can't eat it.'

So we carried the carcass out into the open and
shaved off its bristles with cutthroat razors and
hot water. Then Jean and the slaughterer started on
the *charcuterie*, and I carried the slabs of meat, the
chops, the ribs, the cutlets, the lights and all the
rest of it down to the kitchen, where the women
were waiting. Jean went off to salt the hams and

twist the nerve and muscle out of them, and I
stayed on to help in the kitchen, where there was a
big fire going with *marmites* of boiling water over
it. I listened to the women chattering away,
exchanging village gossip while they worked.

Before he left, the slaughterer slapped me on the
back. 'First pig?' he said. 'Well, you'll have fresh
pork for your dinner today, I know Jean. Cheer up.'

Killing the pig didn't turn me into a vegetarian. I
just sat abstractedly over my pork chop at midday,
thinking how good it was and finishing up every
scrap of it, cutting back to the bone with my big
pen-knife and sucking the marrow reflectively out of
the end of the bone. Yet I still wondered how it
must have felt to take ten minutes to die.

'You did all right, you know,' Jean said as we
started off for the vineyards again at half-past one,
to prune.

'Not as well as the pig did,' I said.

'We'll do another one next Monday,' said Jean
cheerfully. 'There's seven to go.'

Winter at Duéjouls, alone. I stand at the window
with my back to the empty room; I have sold all the
furniture that Margo didn't take. I watch the rain
attack across the mountain opposite, slashing the
leaves off the poplars by the stream. Tomorrow I
finish the *vendange* at the Champagnacs', the grapes
black and beautifully iced with a frost that turns
your fingers blue. Yesterday I cut my hand with the
knife, feeling neither the hand nor the knife. I
poured wine on the cut, better than iodine. It'll be
difficult loading the tubs full of grapes onto the
trailer. The trailer will be solid ice. The wine will
be awful. Water. The Champagnacs are the only

people who leave the *vendange* till the middle of November.

But this cold will pass. The woodlice will come out of the walls again with the spring rain; the snails will sail slowly through the young weeds on the path. There will be warm, wet mornings dark with cloud, and I'll be out with my plastic bag and a stick to get a free dinner of snails, the *petit gris*. I'll put them to fast for nine days with a sprig of thyme, then clean them till they spit with vinegar and salt, boil them out of their shells and cut the shit off them, then do a cold garlic butter with parsley and eat them off the special plates that Margo bought in the market. I shall eat them by candlelight and pretend it's a dinner party. I shan't put the radio on; it talks about nothing but war.

I listen to *France Musique* on the rare occasions when they stop playing Mozart and Haydn or some teaspoon concerto in T minor.

I shut my eyes and it is summer and Margo is back again, sitting out on the terrace with me. She is getting tanned, wearing the straw hat with poppies on it that she bought in the Nouvelles Galeries.

Did it happen? Before Barbara, did anything ever happen? Impossible—everything is impossible.
Time plays such tricks—but why on me?

There was a silence on the tape. Then Staniland continued on a new tack:

What am I going to do about my stepson? I can't go on giving him money, I haven't any more. I gave him that five hundred when I borrowed on the equities, and then that other three. I've got to think of Charlotte. Margo, too. Margo has the house at

Duéjouls for her lifetime, I've seen to that. If
she sells, she just has to share the money with
Charlotte. After all, Charlotte's my flesh and blood—
not like Eric. Margo shouldn't have made that row
at Planet; she thought I'd just pissed off and left her
in the shit. But I hadn't. I'd made all the
dispositions I could. I'm broke, and I can't make
any impression with my writing. It isn't my fault
that people don't want to hear things straight. I
can't work miracles.

I put on the next tape, which started:

Eric takes me for a pushover, a softy. Maybe I am
one. But he's ruthless. I know he can't get a job;
but he sees the world's in a mess and he takes
advantage of the situation by lying in bed all day.
He's also a drug addict. Okay. But I'm not responsible
for him anymore—he's twenty-three, it's up to
the state now. It's not up to me—not up to his
mother, either. Poor Margo—I've heard that if
he's not after me for money, then it's her turn. But
she's not well off. She has to take in men to make
ends meet.

The player fell silent again. I thought: Of course, I'll trace
Margo in the end, but it could take a long time. Suddenly
Staniland broke in again and said:

I fell bad about her, I suppose I ought to go
round to Callow Street one of these days, but I'm
afraid there'd be a scene like there was at Planet. I
wish I could find someone who would listen,
instead of just a tape. Barbara? Barbara's no
bloody good. When I tried to tell her about Margo
she just interrupted me and said, well, your

ex-cow decided she wanted to play it on her own,
so why don't you leave her be?

Well, there was me to listen—though, true, it was too
late. I switched the player off and looked at the time; ten to
seven in the evening, a fine evening. In my early days I
had worked at Chelsea nick—the prison. I shut my eyes and
spread Chelsea out in a mental map. Callow Street was
short; it ran north to south between Fulham and Elm Park
Road. But there were a lot of flats in it. In fact, it was
nearly all flats. But I wondered if I might have some luck
for once and just find the name on one of the street doors.
    I was already down in the street by that time.

18

'Mrs Staniland? Margo Staniland?'

'Yes, that's me.'

She had probably been a pretty woman with red hair and smooth breasts, but she wasn't anymore; she seemed to have clouded over and shifted out of focus. The half smile had once been seductive; now it was vague. Her right eye was bloodshot. She had a kind face, with intelligence in it; but it didn't look as if she used that anymore.

'I don't think I know you.'

'I'm a police officer,' I said. 'I was wondering if I could come in.' I thought: Does she know he's dead? And does she care?

'I was just going out, actually,' she said. 'But of course if—' She gestured behind her into the dark flat.

'I won't take up much of your time.'

'It's all right, I was only going to meet a friend for a drink. Over at the Water Rat by World's End, do you know it? Just a drink to pass the time.' She led the way into the sitting-room, dark even on this early summer's evening. The room faced east. She sat down on the sofa and indicated the armchair. 'Well? What have I done?'

'Nothing.'

'Well, then?'

When I didn't answer at once she said: 'It's strange,

hardly anyone calls me Mrs Staniland anymore. I reverted
to my maiden name quite a while ago.'

'But you were married to Charles Locksley Alwin
Staniland?'

'Yes, that's right.'

'I'm afraid I have to tell you something unpleasant,' I
said. 'Just try and take it easy.'

'He's dead,' she said flatly. 'I knew it.'

'Knew it?'

'Well, I dreamed it. It was a horrible dream.' Her fingers
started to pick at each other in a busy, meaningless way,
then she fell back in the sofa without crying. She was silent
for what seemed a long time. Then she said: 'Was he
murdered?'

'I'm afraid so.'

'I'm not surprised,' she said. 'It was all in the dream. He
reached out for me the way he used to, then his face
suddenly turned shapeless. I dreamed it on Friday night,
and I was only just recovering.'

'He died on Friday. Look, let me get you something.'

She shook her head. 'No. Just tell me everything you
know.'

I did and then said: 'You might be able to help me catch
whoever's responsible. Are you up to talking about it?'

'Yes,' she said. 'The shock won't hit me for a while yet.
Not till after you're gone.'

'He had enemies,' I said.

'Did he, *did* he?' she said, nodding. She jerked her head
up at me and declared: 'Well, I loved him.' She started to
talk too fast: 'The trouble with Charles was that he shot
past everyone; he went like a meteor. I loved him as best I
knew how, but he kept breaking away from me. He was
always looking forward. Always doing it! How am I going
to tell my daughter? Charlotte always said he'd come back!
I ought never to have left him, but he didn't give me any
choice. Quarrel, quarrel, analyze, no money . . .'

She burst into tears; they made a dreadful noise in her throat, like someone raking gravel on a road. When there was a lull she snatched up her bag, hunted in it and produced a crumpled snapshot. She held it out to me. 'That was him holding Charlotte's hand back at Duéjouls, where we lived in France. She's ever so like him, isn't she?'

'Now take it easy.'

'It's like the tragedy of the whole world in a little glass,' she said. 'Great things are all smashed to pulp, and none of us who are left have the spirit to carry on.'

I didn't say anything.

'I want to talk about him,' she said, as if I'd told her not to. 'I want to. This wouldn't have happened if I hadn't left him. A stupid quarrel. Oh, yes, I loved him. He was a great man. He wouldn't allow himself to be recognized. I knew. He was engaged in a kind of *work*,' she said desperately. 'I should have just followed him and tried to understand, instead of making us argue and quarrel. But I was angry at him because he seemed to me to be so wasted, working on the land.' Her face had lost its shape and was red and ugly. But her eyes were beautiful, a dark grey. 'I've got a little money,' she said, 'I'd always have looked after him. I never really cared what he did or where he went, as long as he came back to me.'

'I think he was pretty destroyed when you and Charlotte left,' I said. It was a stupid thing to say on the face of it, but I had a feeling it would make her feel better and it did, anyway for a while.

'Yes, I was best for him'—she nodded—'no other woman would ever have treated him right. He used to tell me that. There was nothing we couldn't discuss together.' She went on: 'I didn't care how often he got drunk as long as he didn't get hurt. I'm guilty, you know. It wasn't till after Charlotte and I had gone that I realized how badly he had needed us. He was the best and sweetest man I ever had.

I've had lots, but he was the only one who touched me. Best lover, best and sweetest man—and don't let people tell you anything different, because plenty of them will try. And he was generous. Too generous. I've never been mean about money, but he was something else.'

'I'll get to the bottom of his death, Mrs Staniland,' I said.

'Maybe, maybe,' she said dully, 'but it won't bring him back to me. I'll always wait for you, Charlie. Never back! Never, never, never, never back!' After a while she said: 'Let me have him when you're finished, I want to bury him myself.'

'Don't worry,' I said, 'I'll see to it.'

'I can afford it,' she said anxiously. 'I've got this money, it's in the post office. I can look after the expenses. See? I'll show you my post office book; I've got the money, I can prove it.'

'There's no need for that at all.'

After another timeless pause in the darkening room, she said: 'Someone will have to tell my son, Eric, and I don't see much of him. I don't think I could face it.' She said in a rush: 'Would you do it?'

'Certainly I will,' I said. 'If you'd just give me the address.'

'It's in Soho.'

I copied down the address she gave me.

'Don't be too hard on Eric,' she said. 'A lot of people are.' She yawned suddenly, worn out. 'But Charles was never hard on him.'

'Your son by a previous marriage?'

She nodded. 'Yes, things were very hard for me in those days, with a baby and no husband. You're a police officer. You give me your word you'll tell him?'

'Oh, yes, I promise,' I said.

'Well, thank you very much,' she said, her voice trailing

away, and when I saw that she was asleep with exhaustion, her blotched face buried in the sofa, I got up and left.

I went out into Callow Street, which was filled with golden evening light. The traffic in Fulham Road which made a T with it was jammed solid; what wind there was blew from the south, taking the petrol fumes away with it. I look at my car, noted that someone had run into the front of it while trying to park, and left it to walk down to a drinking club I knew, not from from Hollywood Road.

There were only four drunks in there when I arrived; also an attractive dwarf with big breasts who had once got a Cabinet minister busted. I ordered a ring-a-ding and drank it alone, slowly, at the end of the bar, staring into the glass. I shook my head over it, and the lady attending the bar who was dressed like a paratrooper came over and asked me if I wanted another.

I said I did. My watch said nine o'clock. When I felt better I finished my second drink, paid—though they didn't want me to, on the mistaken grounds that I might do them some good with Chelsea law—and walked up the moth-eaten carpet to the street.

Young people holding each other tight were drifting into the restaurants, and a new moon rocked over the Thames, attended by a single cloud.

19

I parked on a double yellow line in Old Compton Street
and pushed my way into the German pub. One corner
was packed with young men from good homes, the kind
that draw unemployment benefit and do moonlight building
and plumbing work on the side; they wore paint-stained
Falmer jeans, sneakers and T-shirts, and accounted for the
row of bikes on the pavement outside. They were big young
men and were drinking lager. The other customers were
Greeks, Italians, Asians or Maltese. Some of them were
local delicatessen owners and shopkeepers, but most of
them were pimps for the whores lounging around the two
bars; we knew it was a pick-up centre, but we never did
anything about it. It was a pub where the police couldn't
win—sited in just the right spot, with the whores' flats,
the sex shops and a porno cinema opposite. Also the
governor's kickbacks for copping a deaf 'un were too big.
The brewers had good legal advice too—the best. So we let
it go and just felt a collar or two from time to time
without making a lot of fuss about it.

When I ordered a lager I had to shout. 'Just Like a
Butterfly Does' and 'Woman in Love' roared out of the
jukebox, which was surrounded by girls (most, though not
all of them, black) and by punters, most, though not all of
them, hesitant, and none of them very appetizing. I drank

some beer, then carried my glass over to the group of young men.

'Evening,' I said pleasantly. 'Anyone here seen Eric?'

'Eric the Knack, you mean? No, he's not in tonight.'

'He's broke,' said someone. 'He's out grafting.'

'He couldn't graft his way out of a wet paper bag, Eric couldn't.'

'Pity, I've got something for him,' I said.

'Money?'

'Why not?'

'Well, you could try his pad. You a friend of his?'

'I'm sort of like his uncle,' I said.

'Eighteen, Petworth Street, third floor. This end of Berwick Street market.'

'I know it,' I said. 'But I thought that building was condemned.'

'Well, it is,' said the young man I was talking to. 'It's a squat.'

'You're not a writ-server, are you?' said the boy next to him.

'Certainly not.'

'Not from the council, either?'

'Not a chance.'

'Well, if it's really money you've got for him, he owes me a tenner.'

'And me! He's into me for fifteen quid.'

One of the young men said suddenly: 'God, I fancy that black bird over there, the one with the sequins.'

'Bet you the next round you don't go over and tell her.'

The one who fancied her blushed violently under his short fair hair. 'Do what?' he said. 'No way.'

'Here,' I said, 'why don't I introduce you to her?'

'Oh, no. Really. I just sort of fancied her, that's all.'

'You never know,' I said. 'It's the sort of relationship that might mature.'

'No, honestly.'

I knew her by sight. She called herself Gloria Lovely, and I had come across her years before when I was with the Vice Squad. I just hoped she didn't remember my face, but she saw so many faces in her line that I doubted it.

'Hello, Gloria.'

She put her sweet martini on the bar. 'How did you know my name?' she said suspiciously.

'Through a friend. Do you know Eric the Knack?'

She was a bit drunk. She didn't look as if she had the kind of liver that could manage too many sweet martinis, and she was on grass as well. 'The one that can't get it up, you mean? Thin? Bad teeth?'

'That sounds like him.'

'I know him,' she said broodingly, 'he owes me a fiver. He was sick in the bed the night I had him, *and* he hadn't got all the money. I said I wouldn't get him razored for it this time.' She sighed gustily. 'I don't know why, I never learn.'

'There's one of those boys over there badly wants to meet you,' I said.

'Really?' she said, arching her eyebrows, which she had done orange to match her hair. 'What? One of those virgins over there?'

'They've got to start some time.'

'Yeah, but why with me?' she said bitterly. 'They're all skint.'

'Oh, come on. You've nothing on over here. There's no harm in it, and they'll buy you some drinks at least.'

'I suppose if I've got to, I've got to. But if a real punter shows up, they've had it.'

'They know that,' I said. 'That's in the standard contract.'

'How many of them are there? What, all that lot? What are they gointer do? Gang-bang me?' She looked at me. 'I'm not sure I don't fancy you better.'

'Not me. I'm married with three kids.'

'You mostly are.'

'I couldn't afford it anyway. I've got a mortgage to cope with.'

Something clicked in her eyes. 'You ain't fuzz, are you?'

'Christ, no. Whatever gave you that idea?'

'I don't know. It's just that I can usually spot it.'

'No sweat,' I said, 'I work on the office side of British Rail.' I took her by the arm. 'Come on, Gloria. That's a Latin name, did you know?'

She came reluctantly. 'I reckon it's you older guys always get it up better.' She added: 'Not that it matters much either way, I suppose, as long as they ain't *sick*.'

We joined the young men, and I said: 'Okay, this is Gloria, who's going to buy her a drink?'

'What'll you have?' said the one with fair hair eagerly.

'A double brandy,' she said with a lethargic shrug. When he had gone off to the bar she said to me: 'His accent comes right out through his pants, don't it?' After a pause she added: 'You really know Eric the Knack?'

'That's right.'

'Ain't none of my business, but you got funny friends.'

'What's funny about him?'

'A woman wants to be careful with Eric,' she said. 'He's strictly negative, no-go, no-no-land. He likes to do strange things to a girl.' She thought hard and then said: 'You know? He's exploded like a tape recorder when you put too much juice through it. Like burnt out.'

20

Petworth Street was no distance from the pub, and I soon
found number eighteen; it was the door that banged in the
dark wind and had a pile of costermongers' garbage three
feet high beside it. The door banged because it didn't lock,
and it didn't lock because the traders used the street-level
passageway for parking their barrows and empty crates. I
stood at the foot of the stairs in the gloom for a minute,
then got my flashlight out—where would anybody be in
modern London without one? I looked for a push button
to light the cement stairs that yawned in front of me; there
was one, but it didn't work. On the inside of the street
door was a wire basket full of mail. It looked like disagreeable
mail, the kind that arrives in buff envelopes, and evidently
nobody ever read it, because it looked as if it had been there
a long time. I looked through it all the same, but there
was nothing for Eric. After climbing three floors' worth of
stairs—two doors to a floor, one left, one right—I reached
the third floor. It had two kicked-in doors on the landing,
both toilets, one with a broken cistern and no seat. The
whole building smelled bad. At the end of the landing a
green rail ran across a wide, unglazed aperture. I leaned
out over it and looked down into the well of the building; at
the bottom lay some rotten bedding and a wrecked bike.
There were the same two doors facing each other at the

118

end; the left-hand one had a line of light running under it
and gave off the sound of rock. I went up to that door and
banged on it. There was a noise of breathing through the
thin wood planks, and when I banged on it again a reedy
voice shouted: 'Who're you?'

'It's me, Eric.'

'I don't know your voice. I don't know you.'

'Maybe not,' I said, 'but you've been waiting for someone
like me to call.'

'I'm not opening up!'

'That's a drag,' I said. 'It means I shall have to come back
with the help.'

'You can't be from the council, not at this time of night.
Look, what do you want?'

'Open up and you'll find out. Come on. You'll have to
sooner or later, and the more bother you give me, the
more you'll get into.'

He got the point. I heard steps shuffling over to the door,
and a hand fiddled with the Yale lock. When the door
opened a crack I moved in. 'Thanks,' I said. 'What a lot of
fuss.'

Eric was tall, thin, and ill-looking. He was about twenty-
five and did have rotten teeth. He didn't look much like
his mother, except that his hair, what there was of it, had a
reddish tinge. Behind him the music roared out:

> *I like to rock all day!*
> *I like to rock all night!*

'Turn that off,' I said, 'I want to talk to you.'

He turned it down and said: 'What about?'

'About your stepfather, Charles Staniland.'

'Well, what about him?'

'Well, he's dead.'

'As if I fucking cared,' he said. 'Who are you, you cunt?'

'I'm a police officer,' I said. 'And watch your tongue.

One more slip like that with it, and I'll tear it out of your head.'

'Let's see your identification,' he said in a world-weary voice.

When I showed it to him, he said: 'Oh, Christ. Look, I'm worn down, man, I'm strung right out.' He had a voice as thin as the rest of him; it seesawed up and down like an out-of-tune violin. 'I'm too old for life, too old for the gigs, man—no one lasts for ever.'

'You certainly don't look as if you were going to,' I said. He didn't quite make sense yet; I thought his indifference to me, to Staniland's death, meant that he was on his way down from a trip of some kind. But I didn't care; we had any amount of time. 'How old are you?'

'Twenty-four. Shows, doesn't it, dad?'

'Yes, it looks as if you'd lived,' I admitted, 'only the film seems to have been run through mostly backwards.'

'Oh, well, you gotter live. I'm at the age where a man's gotter live, gotter enjoy himself. You gotter get through it somehow. It's hell, it's strictly hell, but that's how it crumbles, dad.'

'You want to get your valves ground in a bit, son,' I said. 'I'm forty-one, but I could bounce you up and down like a rubber ball.'

'Anyone can use insults or violence,' he said with trembling disdain, 'especially if they're fuzz.'

'Quite,' I said absently. I was looking round the room. There was a table with the dirty remains of a frozen meal on it, shepherd's pie for one, and a segment of Mother's Pride, two chairs and a bed covered with screwed-up army blankets; a soft-porn mag lay on the chair cushion that stood in for a pillow.

I looked Eric up and down. He wore a brown, flowing robe like a monk's, the hem of which, as he sat down, he tucked up round his groin, displaying a lot of white, apparently boneless leg and then, far away where his feet

were, sandals which had died slowly, perhaps while hitching
a ride. He produced, out of the folds of his cassock, a
plastic wallet which proclaimed that it had once contained
Dutch tobacco. It was held shut with a rubber band in
which a lighter acted as a tourniquet; he twisted the lighter
round in the band as he stared at me until it seemed
bound to snap—which it did, showering a brown detritus
over the floor.

'Shit!' he said, bending down.

'Is it?' I said, picking some up.

It was. He giggled on a high, unreal note, but I wasn't
going to bust the poor little sod; I hadn't the heart unless
it came in handy as a means of holding him for something
else. I could see he had done some porridge as it was,
because it said so on his left arm, which was tattooed
'Wandsworth I Love You'. But I was investigating a much
greater tragedy than Eric. Eric might be all right for as long
as anyone with his problems can be. He might even settle
down in the country somewhere for a while on some
reforming maiden's money and sit under a tree making
cages out of twigs while she uncomplainingly hoed the
garden in a glow of sweat, martyrdom and packet soup.
On Sundays her middle-class mum and dad would come
and gaze at them helplessly for the afternoon while she
hoed and he giggled, and then depart in the family motor
not looking at each other, but staring wordlessly over the
gears. Then one day, for any reason or more likely none at
all, the relationship would snap abruptly, perhaps making,
if there were some violence, twelve lines of print on page
three of the *News of the World*, accompanied by a smudged
photo with the background of weeds and a potting-shed.

'I want you to tell me all about your relationship with
your stepfather,' I said.

'There's nothing to tell.'

'Oh, I don't agree,' I said. I watched him desperately
trying to pick his pot up off the floor. He was too idle to

get down on his knees for it, but tried to do it bending from
his chair. 'Let's get back to reality, shall we? Your
stepfather's been murdered. Murdered, do you understand?'

'Yeah, yeah, I read you.'

'You'd better have a look at this.' I said. I produced the
morgue photograph of Staniland and handed it to him.
"Particularly as you're a relative.'

He looked at it. 'Christ,' he said, his voice cracking, 'is
that really him?'

'It was. People like you don't think about death much,
but that's what it can look like.'

'Okay, okay,' he said. He seemed to have shrunk.

'You wouldn't know anything about it?'

'Who, me? Christ, no.'

'It's come as a complete shock?'

'Course it has! Christ!'

'Why did somebody have to die to get you off the hook?'

'He didn't! He must have gone and done it. He was
upset after he broke up with my mother! He was in a
state over my half-sister! I never gave him any sweat!'

'Oh, come on, Eric,' I said woodenly. 'You can do better
than that. I'm going to lean on you now. What did you do
with that money?'

'Money! What money? I don't know what you're talking
about!'

'Yes, you do. He gave you money.'

'I don't have to tell you that.'

'Yes, you do. You have to tell me everything.'

'I can't remember.'

'Well, we'll wait together for as long as it takes you to
remember. You've got a habit, haven't you?'

'Okay, so you saw the pot on the floor.'

'It's a more expensive habit than just pot, Eric. What is
it? Cocaine? Heroin?'

'Why? Are you gointer bust me or something?'

'I can't be bothered. If I wanted to I could spend my life

busting you pimply marvels. But I could hold you on it, pending another charge, it depends on you. You'd find yourself on remand over at Brixton in no time, and you don't want to do any more bird, do you? Last time it was just for thieving, wasn't it, but this time it'll be more serious; they'll throw the book at you harder, Eric, a lot harder.'

'Look, if you're going to bust me, bust me. But I don't know anything about my stepfather's death.'

'You're sticking to that?'

'I am.'

'If you're telling the truth that's one thing. But if you're not, Eric, you're being an A1 prize jerk—you'd be safer telling me the truth. You'd be safer in the nick than you would be on the streets. Have you got a photograph of yourself, by the way?'

'No.'

'Yes, you have. You've got a passport, I checked.' I held my hand out. 'Give me the passport, Eric. I want the photograph.'

He rummaged in an overcrowded drawer and finally produced it. I turned to the photograph. It wasn't a very good likeness, but it would do. I put the passport in my pocket. 'Thanks,' I said. 'Now, I think you're lying to me, Eric; I think lies come naturally to you. But what I'm going to do is show this picture around among certain people, and if I find that you're known to them, God help you, son, do you see?'

He swallowed. 'I move around a lot,' he said. 'An awful lot.'

'Well, it's a matter of where,' I said, 'and who with. You go down to South London often?'

'No.'

'Sometimes, though?'

'I go everywhere sometimes. I move around a lot, I keep telling you.'

'All right,' I said, 'let's leave that for now. Let's go back
to that money of your stepfather's. You spent that money
on your habit, didn't you, Eric? Sometimes it was pot, but
more often it was maybe a little heroin if you needed a
nice strong kick.'

'I've never touched horse!'

'Come on,' I said, 'I don't have to look for the punctures
to tell that you shoot up. Your friends call you the Knack,
don't they?'

'Some of them do.'

'What have you got a knack for, I wonder, apart from a
needle? Nothing very much, I shouldn't think. I wouldn't've
thought you were into birds very hard, for instance—I've
heard it said that you're not all that hot in the sack, Eric.
But if you're turned on the whole time that's hardly
surprising. Spending other people's money, is it? Come
on, talk. I'm beginning not to be very fond of you, Eric,
which as far as you're concerned is bad news.'

'Look,' he said, 'go easy, will you? I admit I'm muddled
and confused. The psychiatrist said it was because I never
knew my father.'

'You didn't do too badly with your stepfather, though.
You did as well with him as a lot of kids would've done
with a real father. You had a decent education, I can tell;
you've got one of those classless accents that you get in
expensive schools these days. Who paid for it, Eric? What
school was it, Eric?'

He told me. It was one of those schools for the delinquent
dropouts of the middling well-off to rich. It turned out
flops, would-be revolutionaries, drug addicts and trendies
by the score; I'd had to deal with its products on other
occasions.

'Did your mother help with the fees? Oh, come on, Eric.
It's so easily checked; I've only got to ask the school.'

'No, I tell you, he paid for everything.'

'He spoiled you, did he?'

'I suppose you might call it that.'

'You should get your teeth seen to,' I said absently. 'People shouldn't let themselves go like that at your age.'

'Well, my stepfather wasn't much of an example, always drunk.'

'You didn't like your stepfather much. Not really, did you? No matter what he'd done for you.'

'He didn't like me, either.'

'Well, he must've a bit,' I said, 'otherwise he wouldn't have given you that five hundred quid, would he?'

'How the hell did you know about that?'

'Don't bother about the details, I just know you had it. I also know it wasn't all you had. You had the two cheques, one for five hundred and the other for three. You pretty well cleaned him out, didn't you?'

'No, I didn't.'

'Yes, you did.'

'Well, if I did, I didn't know I was doing it.'

'How did you get the money out of him, Eric?'

'What do you mean, get it out of him? I told him I needed it, so he let me have it.'

'Soft touch, was he?'

'That's right.'

'You know, Eric,' I said, 'I find life so strange sometimes, when I'm talking to liars especially. What you really said to him was, Give, or else. You knew bloody well he couldn't afford it. You forced him to go to the bank and raise it. You made his life hell for him until he did go to the bank.'

'I didn't!'

'You're lying again,' I said. 'You're an absolute chronic liar, Eric. What I really want to know is how you forced him.'

He didn't say anything.

'Well, I'll tell you what I think. I think you said to yourself, he's a drunk, he's an easy touch, he's weak and

he's easily frightened. I think you put the boot in, Eric. I
think you took a few other little knackies round with
you, and I mean to find out who they were.'

'I didn't take anybody round!'

'I think you did, and the reason why I think it is because
you've got no guts. You couldn't even square up to a
middle-aged alcoholic without sending out for help. But you
know what they call that in a court of law, Eric? A
prosecuting lawyer would call that demanding money with
menaces, and it carries five to seven years' porridge if you
go down. You shouldn't have taken cheques from him,
that's where you went wrong. Because you had to endorse
the cheques and it will be very simple to establish that the
endorsements were in your handwriting even if you used
a false name.'

'I tell you he gave me the money of his own free will.'

'No court's going to believe that. We're talking about a
murder, Eric, and you've got a record, also a motive.'

'Christ, you're trying to fit me up for this!'

'You fitted yourself up for it. And while we're on the
subject of money, by the way, there's another three
hundred quid still missing. Did you get that as well?'

'No! Eight was the lot. Honestly!'

'I wonder,' I said. 'I bet you were into your stepfather
every time you got short of moonfeed.'

'It wasn't like that, I tell you.'

'I think it was. I don't think you could find any way of
raising money except from your stepfather. You haven't
the guts to graft, get a job, work on a building site,
anything like that. No. But darling Eric has to have his
moonjuice just the same. Only the knack ran out in the end,
didn't it? You couldn't put the bite on any harder; your
stepfather didn't have any more money. I'll bet at first you
came on like no end of a wag over at the pub, for
instance, flashing your stepfather's money about. That's
how you really came to be called the Knack, wasn't it? I

wouldn't be surprised if you invented that name all by
yourself. God, I tremble with pride for you, Eric; you
make me go all gooey."

'I keep *telling* you—'

'But you weren't prepared to try the famous knack on
anybody else, were you? No, because anyone with any
balls would have told you to fuck off, and you'd have burst
into tears, just like you're about to do with me. You're
like a sinister little boy, Eric; every time the beastly horrid
sand-castle falls in you burst out crying and try and kick
someone smaller than you are. I bet you think of yourself as
the detritus of your society—it's a good excuse for a
wallow in self-pity. But all you are, Eric, is just a wanker.
What you did with your mates was start roughing your
stepfather up a little, and then it all went too far, didn't it?
Didn't it?'

'No!'

He folded up his chair, a ridiculous spectacle in that
stupid robe, and gazed at me blearily through his tears.
He shook uncontrollably and looked like something nasty
that had been shot in the face. 'He gave it so easy the first
times,' he said. 'There was nothing to it.'

'And then after that there was more to it, and you lost
your temper and then you roughed him up, and then it
went too far and everyone had a go and you killed him.'

'No, it wasn't like that!' he sobbed. 'I didn't kill him, I
didn't, I didn't. I didn't get anything out of him the last
time. And I was on my own with him and I didn't touch
him—I reckoned I'd about got all I was going to out of
him.'

'Maybe he was sober that time,' I said bleakly. 'So you
tuned him up the second time round, is that it?'

'Well, he sort of fell over, yes.'

'You sort of pushed him around that time until he sort of
fell over, you mean.'

'All right, then, yes. But it was really easy before, the first time.'

'Yes, it was easy the first time because he was the kind of man who would give anybody anything if he had it. Your mother told me that.'

'My mother's just a whore!' he shouted through his tears.

'Well, true or false,' I said, 'you're the last person to make judgements about people. I believe you not only killed your stepfather, Eric—but look what you did to him. Look at this photo again.'

'I didn't!'

'How hard did you hit him, Eric? To start with, when he told you he couldn't give you the money?'

'Just a slap! I don't know! Just a couple of slaps!'

'Because you were desperate for your moonfeed, and you were skint, and you hated and despised him anyway.'

'Yes, all right, but I didn't kill him!'

'Well, I'm not sure, Eric.'

'Sure of what?'

'Sure whether my proper course wouldn't be to search the place and then, maybe book you on a hard drugs charge, also grievous bodily harm for a start, and take you across to the Factory so you can repeat what you've just told me over there.'

'What, the Factory?' he moaned. 'Poland Street? Christ, I might as well top myself and have done with it!'

'Oh, it's not as bad as that,' I said, 'though of course you might get a bit of slap and tickle if you didn't cooperate. Whereas I'm not going to touch you, so you've got this last chance to tell me what really happened.'

'Look, I didn't kill him, I've told you twenty times. I swear it. If only he hadn't sent me up—'

'And you hadn't been on moonjuice—'

'No, it was because he sent me up. That's why I slapped him.'

'Well, I've heard he had a sharp tongue,' I said, 'and in

your case it was well justified. Also I've turned up your record, Eric; you seem to have been in trouble with the law since you were in shorts.'

'I'm disturbed, I tell you. What I need's a psychiatrist.'

'Oh, Lord Longford'll find you one of those quickly enough, don't worry. But you maintain that you weren't sufficiently disturbed to kill your stepfather, just slap him around. Not even on moonjuice, Eric? Or deprived of moonjuice?'

'No, Christ! I didn't! I couldn't!'

'It's frightfully weak, Eric. Frightfully weak. You know, you could go down for this, son.'

'I could never have done all those injuries to him! Don't you see?' he screamed. 'I wouldn't have had the *strength*!'

'But nobody's saying you were alone,' I reminded him. I got out my notebook. 'Let's start by having all their names.'

'I couldn't! They'd kill me if I squealed on them!'

'I think the best thing in that case, Eric, would be if I took you into custody for your own protection.'

'No! I'd go mad in there! I nearly did last time!'

I put the notebook away, got up and said: 'All right. I'm keeping you on ice, Eric. Now being on ice means what it says. You stay in your fridge here. If I come round to find you any time and you're not here, God help you. If you move out of this pad or, more likely, if you're evicted, you ring this number and let me know where I can find you.' I wrote it down for him. 'It's ridiculously simple. Do you understand?'

'Yeah.'

'I'm very, very serious, Eric. You make one attempt to bolt, just one, and you go straight inside.' I went to the door, had a thought, and turned. 'A piece of advice, Eric. I wouldn't tell any of your mates I've been round; they sound heavy. I wouldn't say anything about this little talk

we've had to anyone. Now don't you think that's good
advice?'

He nodded.

'Well, take it, then.'

But I knew he wouldn't.

21

It was called the 84 Club because that was its street
number in Crispian Road, on the south side of London
Bridge. Derelict or bankrupt warehouses fronted the
river; the area was scheduled to be bulldozed one day for
new development, and then it would become posh. But I
wondered if that would ever happen.

The 84 was the fifth club I'd tried. I'd been working
along the south bank going eastwards, starting at the
Elephant. I hadn't been lucky with the others, and I'd no
reason to think that this one would be any different. Still,
it had to be checked. The place was got up as a horror
museum, with décor done on the cheap. Plastic cobwebs
were sprayed around where no spider would ever have had
the idea, devils and monsters glowed with twenty-five-
watt bulbs inside them, long white bones dangled from the
ceiling, etcetera. The only thing that wasn't simulated was
the damp. The company was mixed in there—black and
white, like the whisky. It was a powerful blend, and I
wondered if the villainous management knew how to handle
it. I had an idea it did.

I stood at the entrance, watching. The floor was packed
solid; I smelled the hard liquor and sweat, sex, and one or
two other things, such as grass.

The heavy inside his box said: 'C'n I help you, Jack?'

'I'm just looking.'

'I know that, Jack,' he said, 'an I'm gointer try you with this one again, c'n I help you?'

'Maybe. I'm looking for a bird called Babsie.'

'I don't care if you're looking for a razor blade up your arsehole, Jack, it's members only here.'

'It's a pity the Tourist Board can't hear the way you clack on,' I said. 'You'd get a lot of coaches here, I should think. Fine old English manners like yours have almost died out in the land.'

'Look,' he said furiously, when the penny had dropped, 'do you want me to come out an round an give you some manners right in the mush?'

'Yes, why not?' I said. 'If you've got a spare face at home.'

He jumped over his counter in one movement. 'Okay, just one more remark like that.'

I produced a fiver, but when he moved to take it I caught him by his little finger. 'If you move I'll break it,' I said. 'And that's really painful.'

'Look, are you a sadist or something? Or just some nut looking for trouble? Anyway, you'll find plenty of it here.'

'No, I'm just fed up with the way you come on,' I said. 'I want to be a temporary member, that's all, and without a lot of yack.'

'Well, why didn't you say so? C'n I ave my finger back, then?'

'Here you are.' I gave him the fiver, too. He had his mouth open to ask for more, but I said: 'That'll cover me for the entrance and a bottle.'

'That's what you fucking think!" he shouted. "A fiver?'

'Well, if that doesn't cover it, I'll have to see your governor about your liquor licence, and I'd better tell you straight away that I'm a Labour MP.'

'Christ, Jack,' he said, backing off, 'I didn't know they went in for unarmed combat over at Westminster.'

'There are a lot of things you don't know,' I said. 'For instance, my name's not Jack.'

I got a ticket from him and pushed my way through to the bar. The bartender may have seen what had happened at the door because he served me quickly.

'What'll it be?' he yelled above the Joan Armatrading.

'Ring-a-ding.'

He uncapped a bottle of Bell's, got a glass and some ice and slapped the lot on the counter; as an afterthought he slid a bottle after them which said Malvern Water on the label, though I had just seen the contents start life in his tap.

'You alone?'

'That's right.'

'You happy like that?'

'For the time being.'

'Otherwise I could've fixed you up.'

'I'll let you know.' I poured a drink and watched the rave-up with my back against the bar. About a hundred couples were sprinting around to the roar of the music. Next to me I became aware of a paunchy, short man whose belt was having trouble holding him in. He might have been forty to forty-five but looked older because of the bags under his eyes, which could have been sewn into his face up at the Ville. The whites were red like the rest of him till you got to his suit, which was black, and he wore a blue tie with a double Windsor knot.

'You lookin for a bird?' he said.

'I'm always looking for them.'

'Me too. I work here, see? Only I'm off duty tonight.'

'Then you know em all,' I said. 'But there's only one I really reckon; she works the clubs up and down round here.'

'Who's that, then?'

'Babsie.'

'Oh, her,' he said. 'Yeah, she's ere somewheres, I seen her tonight.' He gave me a look that classified me. 'You really go for her?'

'I've only looked so far. Why?'

'Nothing.' He thought deeply, frowning in order to concentrate. He was drinking vodka and tonic, and was far from sober. 'Tell you what,' he said finally, 'you got any loot on you?'

'I could go a score.'

'All right—suppose I match that, find Babsie, row in my old boiler, and make it a four? How's that grab you?'

'Sounds okay.'

'Right, I'll go an see if I c'n find Babsie right away.'

I pushed him five and said: 'Thanks, mate, you're doing me a favour.'

He stuffed the note in his pocket and said: 'I'll get into action.' He had a bit of trouble doing that, but finally shot off across the floor, cannoning into several rockers. 'By the way,' he yelled back at me, 'the name's Tom!'

'Okay, Tom.'

'Don't get your knackers caught in yer knickers!'

He zoomed away, did a quarter-ball snooker shot off a big girl in jeans and swerved through a service door. I waited. After a while a woman's voice said in my ear: 'You're not drinking your Scotch.'

I turned to face her. 'No, that's right. Have some.' I banged on the counter for another glass, got it and made her a drink.

'Well, cheers,' she said, 'I'm Babsie.' She looked at me carefully. 'But I don't seem to know you at all.'

'I hope that's going to change.'

'Oh, you do, do you?' She had magnetism. Now that I'd met her, I realized what Staniland had meant. If you were open to her, something coarse and creamy in her flashed out of her and hooked you. I felt rather open.

'You do the clubs down here a lot?' she asked.

'Quite a bit.'

'Funny I don't seem to know you, then. I know most of the regulars.'

'I'm not a regular.'

'Where did you see me, then?'

'Over at the Hard Rock.'

'Then that was a while ago.'

'I could easily fancy you,' I said. 'Very easily.'

'If I'd had a quid for every man who'd told me that,' she said, 'I'd be a rich lady.'

I realized now what Staniland had been through with her. She was tall and blonde with good legs, an even better bottom and big tits, but not grotesque. It wasn't just her face with the bright pointed teeth and the lazy eyelids; it was the flat disinterest with which she looked at men, as if she didn't give a tinker's damn either way.

'You want to rock?' she said.

'Why not?'

She knew how to do it. We danced three or four feet apart. Sometimes I took her by the waist and swung her on the music; she swung easily, never missing a beat, like heavy, oiled machinery. Unlike with machinery, though, electricity snapped at me every time we touched; I noticed that she was insulated against it herself, though. The rest of the floor receded, and the dancers with it. At one point a rocker in black leather came up with an arm out all ready for her.

'Not now, Dave.'

'Oh, come on, Babs.' He looked through me as if I weren't there.

'Get lost, I said.'

I watched him come down in size with interest.

'I'll be seein' you,' he said with veiled menace.

'Try someone else,' she said. 'I'm full up.'

Behind him, one of his mates laughed; all at once I

imagined myself as Staniland in the Agincourt, wondering
what to do about it when Fenton did the same thing.

'Let's dance,' she said to me. The rocker turned his back
on us and went slowly off to the bar with his mates. We
started dancing again.

'You're good,' she said, through the music.

I didn't answer. I thought, Well I've been looking for her,
now I've found her. I saw why Margo Staniland, or any
other woman, had stopped meaning anything to Staniland
once Barbara came on the scene.

In the end we had had enough rock.

Tom and his boiler were waiting when we got back to
the bar. While the four of us were drinking together, he
moved over and whispered in Barbara's ear.

'Nothing doing,' she said. He recoiled and mused for a
bit. He was really drunk now. Then he went back and
whispered to her some more. The woman with him didn't
like it. She had dyed black hair and a wedding ring
crammed over a fat finger. The ring was going through the
kind of test that showed up the weakness of anything you
did in a registry office when half-pissed.

'Look, fuck off, Tom,' Barbara said, 'I don't want to
know.' She said it brutally, and I watched him deflate like
the rocker had, as if she had sliced into him with something
sharp—it must have taken practice. Finally the woman
with him pulled him away; but before he left he picked up
his empty glass and smashed it on the floor.

'Come on, will you?' the woman said, pulling at him,
'you wanter get killed, you cunt?'

'Bastard!' he shouted at Barbara. 'Bitch!'

'You've got quite a way with men, haven't you?' I said
when they had gone.

'What was that again?' she said icily.

'What did he want with you?'

She yawned. 'Oh, him? He just likes a four-decker, can't
get it up otherwise. Who needs that?'

Tom made me understand what Staniland had been made to understand, that the more a man pleaded with Barbara, the more she enjoyed not giving it to him.

'Well,' I said suddenly, 'I've got to be going.'

'Why? You haven't finished your bottle yet. It's early.'

'It was great,' I said, 'but I'll be seeing you. You finish the bottle.' I picked my cigarettes up off the bar.

'Look, let's neither of us finish the bottle,' she said. 'What you and I are going to finish is something else. You got a pad?'

I thought of my dreary flat at Earlsfield. 'I've got this dreary flat at Earlsfield.'

'Old woman waiting up?'

'I hope not. I'm not married.'

'Christ, that makes a change.' She was moving with me towards the exit.

'Look, I'd really like to,' I said, 'but I can't.'

'Why not? Don't tell me you can't get it up either.'

'Oh, no, it comes up all right.'

'What's the problem, then? You said you fancied me.'

'Well, that's just it,' I said, shaking my head. 'I mightn't want to get too involved.'

'That sounds a bit fucking feeble.'

'Go ahead and think I'm feeble, then.'

'I would,' she said, 'only I don't think you are.'

'Me neither.'

'Listen,' she said, 'let's go to my place. It's closer, New Cross.'

'You're in a hell of a hurry. I'm not used to making conquests that fast.'

'Maybe. You've made one, all the same.'

A simian figure in a red jacket came up to us. He had a widow's peak all right, his hair grew all the way down to the bridge of his nose. 'Trouble here?' he said.

'Yes,' she said, without looking away from me, 'you. Fuck off.'

'Easy,' said the man in the red jacket. 'We don't like no arguments in the place.'

'All right,' she said, 'well then, the quicker you get lost the fewer arguments there'll be.'

The doorman came up. 'Watch it,' he muttered to his colleague. He jerked his head at me. 'Geezer says e's a member of Parliament.'

'That right?'

'That's right,' I said. 'I'm one of those battling members.'

'All right, then,' said the man in the red jacket. 'As long as you wasn't annoyin the lady.'

'It's you that's annoying me, Ernie,' Barbara said. When he had gone she said to me: 'He tried to get into my knickers once. Trouble was, I don't like men with hair all over them, even if they are part owners. Still fancies he can get his nookie, though.'

'Who owns the rest of the place?' I said. 'Harvey Fenton?'

Her gaze zipped up like a dagger. 'Why? You know him?'

'I've heard of him.'

'You keep it that way, then, if you know what's good for you.'

'We were talking about nookie,' I said.

'Yes, and you're the one I want it with,' she said. 'So what are we going to do about it?'

'Have it.'

'Converted you, have I?'

'I didn't need converting.'

'You really an MP?' she asked as we went out into the street.

'No.'

22

'Sit down,' said Barbara, when we got in. It was a nice place she had there at New Cross, better than council housing.

'Well,' I said, picking on an armchair. 'Here we are, alone at last.' Yes, it was a nice flat, but it had a neutral feel about it, impersonal. The furniture, the hi-fi were what you bought on the knock, and the lighting was direct and too bright.

'Fix you a drink?' she said.

'Thanks. Not much water. Plenty of ice.'

She came back from the kitchen with a Scotch for each of us and sat in the chair opposite me. 'Well?' she said. 'Where do we go from here?'

'Information, you mean?'

'That's what I mean.'

'I don't know,' I said. 'Why don't you fire a question? But nothing too loaded.'

'Okay, what do you do for a living?'

'That's loaded,' I said.

'Why? Don't you make any money? Or do you make too much?'

'A hundred a week after tax. That doesn't sound like too much, does it?'

'No. You make it straight?'

139

'That's very loaded,' I said, 'or it could be. It isn't in my case. It's straight.'

'I don't mean to pry, really,' she said. 'It's just that with my background I'm sensitive about money.'

'All right,' I said, 'well, let's just say I get by.'

'So I fall in love with a mystery man.'

'There's no mystery,' I said, 'it's just boring.' I didn't want to tell her too much at once. I wanted time to decide on a story. I wanted to keep several options open. 'Anyway, you fall in love bloody fast.'

'Too fast?'

'Itchy pants isn't what they call the grand passion.'

'You bastard!' she shouted. She uncoiled out of her chair and threw her drink at me. The glass followed it. Both missed and sank into the curtain behind me.

'Nothing broken,' I said, 'so you can fix us another. But don't let's waste the next one.'

When she came back with the fresh drinks she had cooled down. 'You're a queer bugger, you are.'

'You mean I'm not what you thought I was in the club.'

'Something like that.'

'You have hidden depths, too.'

'Does that mean you don't trust me?'

'Trust you?' I burst out laughing. 'I wouldn't trust you as far as I could throw this flat. Why should I?'

'So we just fancy each other, and that's it.' I watched her trying so bloody hard to come on like a girl just fallen in love.

'Well, I was let down rotten by a woman before,' I said. 'Long time ago, but still.'

'I'll bet you deserved it.'

'Maybe, maybe not. Anyway, that's some information for you.'

'Well, it looks as if it'll have to do,' she said. 'At least for the time being.'

'I don't want to get my fingers burnt again,' I said. 'I bet

you've let men down in your time. With your looks, you
certainly could have.'

'Listen, why don't we just get to bed,' she said, 'and see
how that works. I'm tired of swapping half-truths.'

'I'll tell you why not,' I said. I decided to sock it to her.
'Because I'm starting to go off you.' I shouted the last bit.
It cost me a lot to do it, but I managed. It cost me a lot
because she had opened her thighs slightly, and from
where I was sitting, opposite her, I could see right up
between her thighs to her white knickers, and it turned
me on hard. 'Look, you know what it is,' I said. 'If you and
I screw just once, you'll go straight off me, you know
that. Don't you, Babsie?'

'Don't call me Babsie,' she said. She said it indulgently.
'That's for the punters. Call me Barbara. And I wouldn't
go off you after just once. It's true I usually do. But not
you, I don't think.'

'Still, you've had lots of other men.'

'Okay, so?'

'What happened to them all? Didn't any of them mean
anything?'

'They weren't up to standard.'

'I see,' I said. 'What's the standard?'

'You are.'

'No,' I said. 'I'm not going to go mad over a woman, and
then she tells me to get lost.' I stood up. 'I'd rather say
good night and leave now.'

After a time she said: 'Sit down. I want a strong man,
and you're it.'

'I'm not strong. I'm just a realist.'

'Same thing. All I know is, you keep hitting me where I
live.'

'You'd better have another drink, then.'

'I'll get them.'

I downed my new one, then said: 'Well? What about this
bunk-up, then?' I knew that, whatever I did, I had to

behave with her in as opposite a way to Staniland as possible. I had to boss her, if I wanted to stay where I was with her. I found it wasn't nearly as difficult as Staniland had made it.

She drank her drink quickly, too. 'All right,' she said, 'let's go, then.'

'It'll have to be quick,' I said, 'I have to be at work by eight.' I looked at my watch; it was a quarter to five. 'Where do we go?'

'Romantic, aren't you?' she said. 'You're enough to sweep a girl right off her feet, the way you go on.'

It was important to flatter her. 'God help any man who tried to sweep you off your feet,' I said. 'He wouldn't crawl out of the ring after round one.'

She laughed; she couldn't conceal her pleasure.

'That's better,' I said. 'Laughter's important, especially if you're in love.'

'I didn't know that.'

'You've been blind,' I said. 'You haven't found out what passion is. You've had a lot of men instead, but you've never really enjoyed them.'

'You're not a million miles from the truth there.'

'Ever had an orgasm?'

'I've heard of it. I don't think I've ever had one.'

'If you had, you'd have known. You might this time.'

'A likely tale.'

'We'll see.'

She was shy when it came to going to bed. She wasn't the kind of woman you could undress in a fit of passion there, right on the sitting-room mat. When I wanted to undo her bra she said: 'Look, it's got to be done properly.'

'Why?'

'Because it's our first time.'

I didn't believe her. We were both acting, and I wondered who had helped her write her script. It was true that I wanted her badly as well, yet part of me was in no hurry—the brain part. The lust I felt for her was also because I hadn't had a woman for so long. I was disgusted with myself. That didn't stop me, but I was lying to her, and I didn't like that. Now I was going to trump the lie by fucking a dead man's woman, so as to trick her into disgorging what she knew about his death. But that didn't make me feel like a knight in white armour; I wondered what the value of truth really was, if getting at it entailed so many lies.

As I sat in my hard-cushioned armchair, nursing a last Bell's while Barbara got ready for bed, I realized that if I'd been a free agent, if it hadn't been for Staniland, his cassettes and his writing, I would either have gone overboard for Barbara, which would have been all too easy for me, or else said woodenly, look, I'm a copper investigating a death, and got insults or silence. I would have felt better if I had, but I had to unravel what had happened to Staniland, and the fact that I interested her physically opened up the best route. Even so I felt dirty, like any double agent. It might take nerve and acting ability to be a double agent, but that didn't get the dirt off.

I heard her moving out of the bathroom into the bedroom, and smelled soap and steam. Then I heard her rustling between the sheets in the dark.

'Come on,' she said. I found I was by the bed, pulling off my clothes in furious haste to get in there with her. My body felt no scruples, anyway.

'Easy, easy,' she said after a while. 'It's happening to me.'

'Are we going to a club again tomorrow?' she said.

'We'll have breakfast, take our time over it, and then decide.'

'I thought you said you were going to work.'

'Not today. I'm taking the day off. I'll go into the office

and explain. I'll have to go in, I've got some work to clear
up, then we'll meet at lunchtime.'

. 'All right,' she said sleepily.

'We'll have lunch together. I'll tell you where we can
meet. Do you like Indian?'

'How did you know I liked Indian?'

'I don't know. Maybe because I like it.'

She said: 'I could almost kill you, you know. I had one.
An orgasm.'

'I know you did.'

'You're not like the no-hopers I usually get.'

'All right,' I said, 'don't say any more now. We'll talk
later.'

'Yes,' she said, 'I want to sleep now; just don't let go of
me till I sleep.'

23

When I got up at seven-thirty Barbara was still sleeping,
her head on her arm, lying on her right side. I left a note on
the pillow telling her to meet me in the Quadrant at one,
and added the address. Then I went out into the river-cold
street and took a cab back to the 84.

I found my car where I had left it, just as a traffic
warden was writing me out a ticket. He was a young
man with mild blue eyes and the beginnings of a
beard.

'Save it, son,' I said, 'it's a police vehicle.'

'That's what they all say.'

'Some of us mean it.' I showed him my identification.

'Well, I've made the ticket out now,' he said. 'It's too late
once I've started making it out. Sorry, Sarge.'

'The man you want to apologize to,' I said, 'is the
Chancellor of the Exchequer. It's him who'll be six quid
out at the end of the financial year.'

'Well, the vehicle wasn't marked.'

'There's a silly reason for that,' I said, taking the ticket.
'It's because a lot of these modern villains can read.'

I drove over to Poland Street and left the Ford in the
police parking lot. Then I went round to the front of the
building and barged in through the main doors just like a
criminal with a complaint. I said good morning to people

145

as I made for the stairs, but they saw me so rarely that
nobody recognized me except the desk sergeant.

I was running upstairs to the second floor where my
office was when I banged into Bowman.

'Christ, it's you,' he said. 'You still on that Staniland
case?'

'Still?' I said. 'I've only been on it four days.'

'Four *days*? You should have had the geezer in half the
time. You'll be working weekends if you don't pull your
finger out.'

'Don't be silly,' I said. 'If you solved them that fast,
they'd start stripping you down for the microchips to find
out how you did it.'

'How are you getting on with it, anyhow?'

'I can't get my proof,' I said. 'You know me—slow,
quick, quick, slow, Mr Foxtrot they call me. That's why
I'm still a sergeant while you're shaping up for superintendent
on the Vice Squad. All I can say is, when it happens,
don't get done for looking at dirty pictures on the taxpayer's
time.'

'You really make me laugh, you do,' Bowman said. 'You
come out with better jokes than a villain.' He continued:
'Now listen, I'm serious for once. You're a good copper—
you can't stay on at A14 forever. Why don't you give it
up and move over to Serious Crimes with us? Do yourself a
bit of good. Come on, I could get you the transfer.'

'No,' I said.

'You hate my guts, is that it?'

'It's nothing to do with that. If everyone only worked
with people they liked, you wouldn't have a police force.
No, I told you, I like being independent, I like working my
own way.'

'Christ,' said Bowman, 'as if I didn't know it—I'm not
sure you wouldn't be better off with M16 or the Branch,
you're so fond of cover. My life, you're too fond of it—you

hardly surface long enough to get a pay rise, let alone promotion.'

'Every time you talk about promotion,' I said, 'you go all starry-eyed like a trendy writer dreaming about a CBE.'

That was what always happened between me and Bowman. We'd start off trying to be nice to each other and then, before you could say Fraud Squad, we'd be at each other's throats again. It was a lucky thing we didn't run into each other too often, as I say; it would probably have ended in murder.

'You stink with the grot of that Staniland case,' he said, sniffing at me. 'You smell as if you'd come straight out of a tart's parlour.' I couldn't tell him what a neat bit of detection that was. 'What I say is, get a transfer over to us. I'll help you—but I can't help you if you won't help yourself.'

'I'm not going to get a flat tyre if I don't make inspector,' I said.

'Just as well,' said Bowman, 'because you've got no chance at all at A14. I can't think of a single man who's made it past sergeant at Unexplained Deaths, and I just don't see why you try so bloody hard.'

'It's because I don't like middle-aged drunks being battered to death.'

'Then if I were you,' said Bowman, 'I'd get hold of the people you've been interviewing by the short hairs and really grip them. Frighten the shit out of them. Somebody must be lying—somebody's always lying. So get some wind in your bellows and give it a bit of puff; the organ'll soon start playing.'

'Yes,' I said, 'but completely out of tune. This is a case where you've got to tease the truth out, not beat it with a club.'

'*Tease* the truth out?' said Bowman. He barked with laughter. 'You'll be at it for ninety-nine years. I get a conviction the quick way. I get results, don't I, Sergeant?'

'Yes,' I said, 'but there's five of you.'

We parted on a bad note, as usual. I went into my office and slammed the door.

I sat down at my desk in Room 205, a pastime I was not fond of. But it was peaceful in there, and I needed some peace. All round me I could hear the Factory pounding away, working. People shouted at each other, the boots of police clerks tramped down the corridor. I spent a quarter of an hour thinking about Barbara with my elbows on the desk and my chin in my hands. I gazed at the police posters on the walls that warned you to look out, there was a thief about, and what to do in the event of the Thames flooding. I stared at the uncomfortable chair that I sat people in to be interrogated, at the Ministry of Works radiator painted sickroom green, and the vase of flowers on the table where another copper sat as evidence of what had been said. Nothing was being said in Room 205 today, and the flowers had been dead for weeks. I didn't even know who had put them there—possibly Brenda, the police constable who gave me looks sometimes. I thought about her legs, which were good, once she'd got her regulation shoes off, but immediately visualized Barbara's body on top of them.

I thought with some bitterness about Bowman. He headed his team at Serious Crimes; he solved his cases practically by committee. I admitted he had to have help; the majority of his cases were headlines in the national press. Yet at the same time he took less individual responsibility. If Bowman dropped a bollock, he could usually blame someone under him, but in any case the shit finally fell on the Commissioner, or a Chief Constable if it was a provincial case. But in my cases, the whole lot fell on me. I accepted that, but it got up my nose at times, especially when I was tired, like today.

Headlines got me back to thinking about Staniland again. There had been eight lines about him in the *Standard* on

Monday, and that was all. The Sundays hadn't touched it—why should they? There wasn't a headline to be got out of him, nothing like 'I Was Raped, Screamed Spanish Waiter', or any of that routine. A middle-aged drunk is found battered to death in some bushes out in West Five. No angle? No espionage? No rake-offs, pay-offs? No thousand-pound roll of dirty fivers in his mac pocket? No sex angle? No weeping girl-friend, kiddies or old mum? I could hear the editors saying, Scrub it, when it came in on the telex. It wasn't as if it were rape, multiple homicide committed by a rampaging nut with a stolen antique battleaxe, kidnapping, vast-scale bank fraud or political mayhem with the SAS and the Branch involved. Every time I thought about the Branch I felt bitter, because I had once applied to join it. I had been accepted and then suddenly turned down after passing the interview without being told why (they never told you things like that). I suspected it had to do with my divorce. People like Bowman didn't know I had ever applied, but it was on my record somewhere—everything was on your record, down to the last time you'd put on clean underwear.

Well, I made the best of it. I was divorced. Exactly. I didn't need the extra money promotion would have brought. I had my flat out at Earlsfield, a motor and a colour TV—what more did a single man want? Besides, as I'd told Bowman, I had the kind of mentality that enjoyed the work at A14. Every so often, too, you turned up something interesting and delicate, starting with something quite banal.

But Staniland wasn't one of those cases.

'Between you and me,' Bowman had said, 'Staniland is one of the most boring cases I ever heard of.'

I didn't agree with him. At least two people, his widow and Viner at the BBC, cared a lot about what had happened to Staniland—three people, if you counted me. For me, Staniland wasn't just another body in the

morgue. Through his writing and his cassettes he was still
alive as far as I was concerned. I had started to think,
dream, almost be Staniland by proxy, even before I had met
Barbara. Now, because of my relationship with her I, like
Staniland himself, was being twisted into a new, more
complex shape.

I knew it was dangerous, but I was becoming obsessed
with Barbara; I could still fall in love with her if I didn't
look out.

I imagined the headline in the *Police News*: 'Detective-
Sergeant Weds South London Club Hostess', and winced.

Pity it would never happen—I'd have asked Bowman to
be best man.

24

I surveyed the lunchtime mob in the Quadrant. The advertising people with their flannels, crew-cuts and executive briefcases stood at the more elegant bar; next to them, but not speaking to them, was the rag-trade contingent over from Great Portland Street. Both armies were attended by secretaries who wittered blondely away at each other across tepid gin and tonics. They received pats on their unisex bottoms from time to time; otherwise they were left to themselves to make their marriage plans. Occasionally the fervent face of a producer, male or female, would pop through the barroom door as though on a spring; those were the people from Independent Television round the corner in Wells Street. Also a newscaster might drift remotely across the scene, too drenched in disasters to be seen talking to just anybody. If such people did stay, however, they ordered democratic halves of lager and talked shop, using well-rehearsed gestures and smiles, aping 'The Upper Classes', a new series that was being run on television by the company in which Lord Boughtham, the Foreign Secretary, held a controlling interest.

My side of the pub was the cheap side, where the fruit machines, jukeboxes and villains were. It was crammed just now with Planet drivers from over the road swilling down Guinness and eating sausage, mash and peas at the

lunch counter. A youth who I happened to know had done
eight for murder stood on his own under the window next
to a space-game, not drinking, not doing anything. His face
was white; he wore his hair cropped and was dressed
completely in black. Even his sneakers he had polished
black. Not only was he a murderer, but he looked like
one, which as a policeman I thought was pretty stupid of
him. On the middle finger of his right hand he wore a big
silver ring shaped like a skull with two paste rubies for eyes,
just in case people still hadn't got the message; all the
other fingers on the hand, and the thumb, inclined towards
it. His eyes slid over me, over all the drinkers; they didn't
rest on anyone, just looked briefly through them. I could
visualize his expression not changing whether he was
ordering a beer or pulling a trigger; the two halves of his
personality were not, and never had been, on speaking
terms. I also noted two well-known tealeaves—thieves, you
know—who were coming up for sentence at Knightsbridge
Crown Court. They were chatting to the elderly homosexual
from the working-class flats in Gosfield Street who bred
Doberman pinschers. The shorter of the tealeaves had been
badly cut in the face and was declaiming drunkenly
through his tears. The cuts were fresh and had stitches in
them; they suggested a broken bottle. He had most likely
squealed on someone, and vengeance had just had time to
catch up with him before they tucked him away in jail.

Barbara came in suddenly. What she was wearing wouldn't
have recommended itself to the change-jingling television
mob, let alone their secretaries. All the same there was a
thoughtful pause when she entered; even the murderer
looked slowly round at her. Her orange dress was wrong for
this side of the river, and her high-heeled slippers would
have looked wrong anywhere except in the 84 Club. She
had tried hard, and it showed. But nobody seemed much
bothered about that; she looked pretty astounding.

'You're late,' I said.

'Okay, okay, but don't let's start the right day off wrong.'

'What'll you have?'

'Aren't you going to give me a kiss?'

'Not in here.'

'All right. I'll have a sweet martini.'

'You're mad to drink those. Women haven't got the liver for them.'

'Listen, are you giving me orders?'

'Yes, if you're my girl.'

'I'm not anybody's girl.'

'Okay, well in that case I won't get you anything. What's the point?'

She went white with rage. 'You've got a fucking nerve,' she hissed. She burst out of the place, with all the producers and textile folk gazing after her. One of the producers said to me: 'I say, old boy, you shouldn't upset a stunner like that.'

'Try bowling more lobs,' I said, 'and button it.'

I drank my beer, waiting to see if she would come back. I knew she would; she was just acting. Behind her act was her body, which only reacted to violence and subjugation; it would always let her down.

She came back after ten minutes, anger simmering under her renewed makeup. 'Why did you treat me like that,' she said, 'you bastard?'

'It's the only way with you,' I said, 'from a man's point of view. If I gave you that much leeway you'd crush me, and I'm not wearing it.'

'Tell me some more.'

'Later, at lunch. Now then, round two—what'll you have?'

She burst out laughing: 'You amaze me—well, I won't have a sweet martini, anyway!'

'Okay,' I said, 'then let's split a bottle of champagne. I feel like celebrating, and you can't celebrate on beer. You know anything about champagne?'

'It's just champagne.'

'No, it isn't. I read that in the *Sunday Times*, but that's all I can remember.'

'You've really got no idea about champagne?'

'How can you expect me to know much about something I've only drunk twice? Anyway,' I added, 'you've no idea about men.'

'Why should I have? I'm a woman.'

I couldn't think of an answer to that, so I said to the girl behind the bar: 'A bottle of champagne. A good one.'

'You mean the Clicko?' she said, bemused. 'Expensive, that is, cost you eight pound twenty.'

'That's the stuff, then.'

The arrival of the champagne caused a strange, almost innocent note to creep between us—it was as if, for an instant, we really were a shy bridal couple toasting each other. She kissed me over our glasses; I shook myself savagely inside. I kissed her back, but it was a very chaste kiss; I had a nightmarish feeling that any plainclothesman over from the Factory watching people from a corner might all too easily recognize me.

'You don't come on quite as hot in the daytime as you do at night,' Barbara said, 'if you'll excuse my saying so.'

'I do better without an audience.'

'Funny, with most men it's the other way round.' She drank some champagne and said: 'You're not ashamed to be seen with me or anything? Who do you think you are?'

'A lover,' I said, 'and I've never been ashamed of anything in my life. I had a very happy childhood.'

'Why've you never got married, then?'

'I was once,' I reminded her. 'But there's no point in going out of your way to be disappointed.'

25

We ate at the Light of India, in the Fulham Road; it was
the best Indian food I knew of in the area, even if it wasn't
cheap.

'I'm having a beef phal,' I said. 'But not you. It's too hot
for you. Have a dupiaza.'

'I'll have what I like,' she snapped, and ordered a
vindaloo.

'Independent, aren't you?'

'That's what you like about me. At least I've sussed out
that much about you.'

'Okay,' I said. 'In that case, why don't we have a prawn
and spinach to go with it? Besides, it's nice and cheap.'

'I will say one thing about you,' she said. 'You have got
style, I don't bleeding think.'

'I've been saving the style up. The money too.'

'What's that supposed to be leading to?' she said coldly.
'A joint bank account?'

'No, a bottle of wine. Know anything about wine?'

'I'd rather have beer with curry.'

'Fuck it,' I said, 'we'll have both.'

When it had all arrived and we were eating she said:
'I'd better tell you something, because when I have it'll be
your last chance.'

'Last chance for what?'

She paused. 'I'm falling in love with you. Have fallen.'
I didn't speak.
'We could just have this lunch, very nice—and then call it
a day.'
'We could,' I said, 'but we're not going to.' We stared at
each other across the table, while the staff stood in the
dim background with their feathery music going and napkins
over their arms, nodding approval. Everyone likes watching
a couple in love.
'I was nothing but a frigid little virgin up till last
night, yet I've had hundreds of men.'
'That's no crime.'
She was instantly alert. 'Crime? That's a funny word to
use.'
'It's a manner of speech. I don't care if you've had a
thousand men. They're all in the past.'
'Not all.'
'They will be from now on.'
'You mean that?'
'I mean it. I've had women too. But it took you to make
me realize they were all the wrong ones.'
She shuddered. 'I love you,' she said with great intensity.
'It's the same with me. Eat up, your food's getting cold.'
'You take a girl's appetite away.'
'Well, I'm hungry.'
'Eat up, then. A lover needs plenty of protein. I read that
in the *Mirror*.'
The head waiter came up. 'Everything to your satisfaction,
sir? Madam?'
I nodded.
'Excuse me, sir,' he said, frowning after a memory,
'haven't I seen you in the restaurant before?'
I turned cold. 'No, I've never been in here before.'
'I'm very sorry, sir. My mistake.' He retreated.
When he had gone Barbara said: 'I wonder who he
thought you were?'

'God knows.'

'He certainly seemed to recognize you. Waiters have a good memory; they have to.'

The first time I had gone into the Light of India was as a young copper attached to Chelsea, to arrest a drunk who wouldn't pay his bill. Then later, when I was with Chelsea CID, I took to eating there off-duty sometimes. I'd had a moustache in those days, which I'd long ago shaved off; that was why he hadn't been sure.

Barbara was saying: 'I think you'd better tell me some more about yourself, things being the way they are. You're still a mystery to me, and I don't like that if I'm going with a feller, why should I? One thing that strikes me, for instance, is that you aren't the kind of man who's really into South London clubs much. You can carry it off, but basically it's not your style.'

I knew what was coming next.

'So just what do you do for a living? Come on.' She spoke flatly.

'I told you before—it's so dull it might put you off me.'

'Not if it's a steady job it won't,' she said. 'I'm up to my eyeballs with hand-to-mouthers. Anyway, let's see if I can puzzle it out. You're bright, and you don't stand for a lot of shit. You like giving the orders, yet you don't come the acid. And you're not rich.'

'I'm certainly not that.'

'Not rich,' she mused, 'but not on supplementary benefits either. No, because you've got this job, at a time when there's over three million unemployed. How long've you been with your firm?'

'Fifteen years.'

'Fifteen years. Always the same firm?'

'Always the same.'

'You're sort of unobtrusive when you want to be, aren't you?'

'It's not intentional.'

'I don't give a fuck about that. It's there.' She shook her
head wonderingly. 'Christ I don't know,' she said.
'Except that it's unbelievable, I'd almost have said I'd fallen
for a fucking copper.'

'Relax, relax,' I said, 'you're way off.'

'Well, okay, come on, then.'

'It's so bloody prosaic,' I said. 'But all right—I work for a
security firm—you know, taking large sums of cash
around in armoured trucks.'

'Which firm?'

I knew she would check, so I said Ashley Security. They
let us use them, and we let them use us—within reason—
and they had my name on the nominal payroll.

She lit a cigarette and closed her eyes against the smoke.
'Still, you work funny hours. You were off last night at
the 84, and you're not working again today, either.'

'Today's special. Tonight too. I got a mate to stand in for
me this morning; that's what I went to the office for.'

'Well, well,' she said, relaxing. 'Ashley Security, fancy.
An ex-boy-friend of mine, he did one of your trucks not a
long while back.'

'I didn't know he was your boy-friend,' I said, 'but you're
dead right, it was a bloke called Lofty Walker in 1980, up
at Edgware. And listen, if you've finished with me, how
about your answering a question or two?'

'I don't want to.'

'Why not?' I said. 'I've come clean.'

'Well, you said your boring job might put me off
you—the same goes the other way round.'

'It's no good,' I said. 'You've got to tell me. We've got to
trust each other—it's hopeless otherwise.'

'I've been mixed up with some funny people.'

'That's okay, I can take it.'

'Well, look, I've done porridge, okay?'

'Okay. What for?'

'It's one not many women go down for—grievous bodily
harm.'

Physically, she looked well capable of it, with her big
shoulders, heavy arms. Beautiful, but big. All it needed
was one of her murderous surges of rage, the trigger. Most
women don't go straight into a battle; they're too frightened
of what might happen to their face. But there are exceptions.
I didn't say anything.

'I did four at Holloway,' she was saying. 'Hollywood, we
call it, and the rest at Askham Grange Open. Are you
sure you still want to go on knowing me?'

'It doesn't make any difference to me,' I said. 'I know
plenty of people that've done bird. So what? Once you've
done it you've done it, and that's the end of it.'

'I was out of an orphanage,' she said. 'No one wanted to
adopt me; I started playing rough at no age at all, and I
was big. I didn't want to work at any crappy job, either,
and I was bored. Angry, too—I reckoned I'd got all the
looks and none of the opportunities. Anyway, one night, I
was out with a bunch of mods (I'd long ago fucked off
from the orphanage), and that's when it happened—we got
in a fight with some rockers on Brighton beach after the
pubs shut. It started because one of the rockers called me a
fucking whore. I picked up this big stone and started
smashing in his head with it; it took three coppers to get me
off of him, I just didn't care. But by the time they'd got
me off of him he was dead, okay? They said for me to
plead self-defence, but the judge took against me the way
I talked back in court, so did the jury, an I was weighed off
for five. So then I appealed against sentence, though the
lawyer said for me not to, and they bumped it up to seven.
Well, the bastards,' she said, 'I did four. I didn't like it,
the open nick up north; I ran away so as to get caught and
sent back to London. I liked Holloway,' she said reflectively,
'I practically run that nick, I even put the shits up the
screws.'

After a pause, she went on: 'It was all the worse, what
that boy said, the one I topped, because it was true.
Boredom, that's always been my worst enemy. School? I
hated it. Anyway, I ran our stream at the comprehensive.
I was in one of the classes where the teachers had to go
round with walkie-talkies so they could call for help if
they got beaten up. Mind, it wasn't that I didn't have
brains—even the teachers admitted that. But I hated the
patronizing way they came on. And I didn't like the way
they thought they could select my knowledge for me—
you can learn a little bit of this, a little bit of that. So I was
all defiance and boredom. Anyway, I started taking my
knickers down the minute I realized that was what the boys
wanted. Mind, I never thought that much of any of
them—I showed them what I'd got to show and said, Okay,
get it up, then, and all they did was go gooey on me, and
I can't respect that. But I thought, maybe it'll give me a
kick. It didn't, though. I just ended up doing it for a
living.'
    'Well, that's over now,' I said. 'Look, I've been thinking it
out while you were talking, and I'll tell you what I think
we ought to do. You know I have to work—we need my
money.'
    'Sure.'
    'Well, I'm not going to go mad while I'm at work,
wondering what you're getting up to, I'm not the type.
Anyway, what kind of relationship would that be?'
    'Lousy.'
    'Right. So it'll be up to you. You don't need to worry
about me—I don't play around. But you do what you
want while I'm out. I don't expect you to stay at home all
day, getting bored. I'm simply going to trust you because,
as I say, I believe that everything worthwhile's built on
trust.'
    'And if it don't work out?'

'Then it'll just be something that wasn't meant to work out.'

'Christ,' she said, 'you're chancing your arm. I've never heard anyone come on like that before; you're a pretty amazing feller, aren't you?'

'It's the only way, when you really look at it,' I said.

'Well, we'll try it,' she said. 'As I say, it'll be the first time round for me.'

'Let's have a brandy, then. Seal it. Make you feel good.'

'Brandy? Christ, we're living it up, aren't we?'

'If we can't do it today, we can't do it any day.'

'Seems a shame,' she said. 'It's always the punters buy me the brandies. Seems silly your paying for them.'

'Wrong,' I said, 'it's worth it. It means I'm not a punter.'

She opened her bag and passed me a tenner under the table. 'They're on me. Whatever's over can go on the lunch. If we're really going to share everything, we might as well get on with it.' When the brandies came she said: 'Look, where are we going to live?'

'Not at my place,' I said, 'that's a racing certainty. It's horrible.'

'You like it over at New Cross? It's only thirty-five a week and there's room for the two of us.'

'You bet I like it. You've no idea how grotty a place looks with just a bloke on his jack living in it.'

'You'd be surprised what I've got an idea of,' she said. 'There was a place I lived in for a while over at Lewisham. Christ, what a terrible little pad that was.' She shook her head slowly.

I knew just which place she meant, but it wasn't the moment for any police work. Looking at her, I began to wonder with trepidation when it would be.

'Okay,' she said, 'what are we going to do next? You seem to be giving the orders these days.'

'That's easy,' I said, waving for the bill. 'We'll go to bed,

then go and have a drink together somewhere when they
open.'

She didn't say no. I kissed her across the table. I smiled
at her. I felt heavy as lead at the strides my deceit had
made—it was like watching an animal toppling into a trap
you had dug for it. I had to remember Staniland,
remember him hard.

Barbara and I started living at New Cross together from
that day on.

26

'Just living,' said Barbara as we lay in bed that night, 'just rotten old living, I've always hated that, it makes me want to puke. Kids, school, smells, Dad working for the council, regular meals, telly in the evening—who needs it? Where's your time for living gone? Well, it's gone, but by the time you realize it you're nothing but a worn-out knitting and washing machine. Then when it's too late and you're fifty and you've got the menopause, you take off your woolly one night and see there's fuck-all left of you except a pair of flabby old tits that no one wants to know about and bulges all over. Even your kids don't want to know you by then; they're grown up, swinging, they've got their own thing going. As for Dad, he's ogling the teenage slag down at the boozer, drinking up, getting all ready to make a scene when he comes in because he feels cheated—of course he feels cheated, the silly old bastard.'

She slammed her legs viciously straight down in the bed. 'I'm not having that,' she said, 'I'm just not having it.' Outside it had begun to rain, the cold sort of rain like the night we had found Staniland; wind tore at the steel-framed window, then changed direction so sharply that the walls shuddered.

'Still,' I said, 'you've got to be middle-aged somehow. You can't stop time.'

163

'Yes, you can,' she said, 'you can die.'

'Easier said than done,' I said. I had seen it too often as a
copper on the beat, at the station, in the hospitals, people
who had tried to top themselves and made a balls-up of it,
and who now might go either way, but come back
crippled if they came back at all.

'No,' she said, 'you've got to be practical about death,
that's all. It's a matter of making up your mind and then
being practical about it.'

'Maybe it's the way I was brought up,' I said, 'but I think
that's wrong.'

'Wrong?' she said, 'who's got the nerve to say it's wrong?
Self-righteous old bastards who wring the juice out of
you? Their wrong isn't my wrong. Your life's your own—
it's no other nosey parker's business. Anyway, I've always
done wrong, I was never any different.'

I looked at her face and saw the shadow over it.

'Doing wrong's no worse than reading people lectures.
People with money telling people with no money what's
right and wrong, that's really wrong—it's always the wrong
people who do it. I should know,' she said bitterly, 'I had
it at the orphanage, then at school, then another dose of it
in the nick.'

'I don't see the two of us growing old together,' I said.

'Oh, I don't know.' She stared upwards with her hands
behind her head, arching her back; it showed off her
powerful arms and the large smooth curve of her breast.
'I've never been in a situation like this one with you and
me before.' She closed her eyes. 'I don't know if I can take
it or not.'

'Why couldn't you take it?'

'I don't like things that go on too long.'

'You mean you want everything out of a relationship, but
not the responsibility.'

'I'll tell you what I mean,' she said. 'I mean you ask too
many fucking questions.'

'Then don't disappoint me by not answering them,' I said.

'You make a habit of asking questions.'

'I've got a brain,' I said, 'so I use it.'

Suddenly the temperature was going up between us. The wind blubbered round the outside of the house and tore through a crack in the window with a whining noise. Just before she balled her fist and hit me in the face I noticed for some stupid reason that the alarm clock beside her said two minutes past twelve.

'Now what are you going to do?'

I got out of bed. I could already feel the bruise coming up at the corner of my mouth, and I sucked some blood in that she had drawn with a ring she had on. 'I'm leaving,' I said. 'It's better for both of us that way.'

'Easier, you mean.'

'More honest.' I started to get dressed.

'So much for love,' she said. 'I never thought it lasted long, but this must be a record.'

'You don't go in for love,' I said, 'only hatred. You're chock-a-block with it, I hadn't realized.'

'It isn't hatred,' she said, 'it's fear. The moment anyone starts digging into me I get afraid, and that makes me a dangerous cow. You're the first man who ever made me react in the sack, you're the first man who's ever got this deep into me. And you're leaving?'

'Put like that,' I said, 'leaving does seem feeble.'

'Well, why don't we have a farewell drink and think it over? The whisky's in the sitting-room.'

When I got back with the drinks she was out of bed. She put her hands on my face and felt the bruise with clumsy, unaccustomed fingers: 'I've never done this to a man before. Am I hurting you?'

'No.'

'I'll put something on it.'

'Whisky'll do,' I said, 'it works every bit as fast as iodine.'

She laughed and fell back on the bed; later on we made love.

Afterwards, when we had uncoupled and she had coughed me out I remembered how Staniland had recorded: 'No effort succeeds with Barbara. No effort I make with her means anything to her, yet I've got to keep making one, like a prisoner in a chain-gang. Don't choke me, Barbara! Listen! Don't—'

Barbara had put the light out. Wakeful, I fingered the bruise on my face, sensed the leadenness of my body and thought upwards into the dark in circles, the darkness measured by her breathing.

I looked at her sleeping, her body caught briefly in the radiance of the headlights from a passing car. Her face was hard in the white beam, and I was sure suddenly: *She knows who I am and why I'm here.*

I couldn't sleep. It was a hot night and the room was too stuffy. I tried in vain to sleep, but found myself thinking of Staniland, as usual. On one of the tapes he had said:

> I want to die but I'm afraid to. I have to accept that when I'm dead I shall start to swell and stink—I can't believe it of this body that I'm so used to. But in my last summer at Duéjouls, death came to the village one day in hot weather; the youngest son of the people down at the castle died of a congestion while he was bathing in the icy water of the Tarn; he was seventeen. Despite the difference in our ages, he was a friend of mine; together we used to dig the sheep-dung out of the vaulted cotes underneath the castle, empty it onto his father's trailer and go and spread it on the fields. He never questioned me. He was too intelligent to ask questions.
>
> The day he died, I went up the same evening. I

didn't want to go up to the castle only three hours
after he had been brought back from the river, but
his brother invited me. I went upstairs; his
parents and some relations stood in the small stone
drawing-room. They wept in the suffocating
darkness, the shutters and windows tight closed.
They switched the light on so that I could see him
for a moment; he was laid out on a bier under a
sheet of muslin, in shirt and slacks, with his hands
crossed on his breast. His hands and face were
pointed and angular, and had turned blue. Then
they turned the light out again. I had taken my hat
off and was wringing it in my hands. His mother
and father threw themselves roughly into my arms
and we all held on to each other and kissed and
wept. 'Why did God let me have him,' his mother
cried, 'when it was for such a short time?' And a
moment later: 'He hasn't moved, he still hasn't
moved.' She hadn't accepted yet that he never
would. Meanwhile, there was harsh peasant whispering
in the dark. One woman murmured in Occitan: 'He
isn't swelling yet, but he soon will in this heat—
it's fifty centigrade out there in the sun.' 'They'll
bury him as soon as the forms are filled in,' a man
said in a loud, comforting mutter. 'Day after
tomorrow for sure.' Meanwhile the boy's father
whimpered quietly. I had never before heard such a
sound from a man as tough as he, and hope never
to again.

I had a casual job in the cemetery at that time
with another man; the regular grave-digger was off
sick. It's hard work digging there, especially in the
summer with the earth hard as cement; it isn't the
kind of work that gets many takers. But we didn't
need to dig this time. To bury the boy in his
family's vault we only needed to move a fairly new

coffin to a different place, because there wasn't
much room left in there. But this coffin had swelled
up with gas inside with a pressure so great that
the gas had smashed several of the planks. Tough
planks they were, too—mountain oak that my
neighbour Espinasse had cut and seasoned and then
taken down to the Vayssières' sawmill; then we
shaped them and planed them. *It was the most
atrocious business for both of us, moving that coffin, but
of course, we managed.*

Of course I shall stink when I die. I shall swell
up like everyone else and there'll be nothing left of
me. Only, like all truth about oneself, it's so hard to
believe, and I couldn't for ten years. But now I'm
all right again and have got my strength back to talk
lucidly into my machine.

Anyone who conceives of writing as an agreeable
stroll towards a middle-class life-style will never
write anything but crap.

27

The following night we were lying awake in bed; Barbara had been silent for a time.

'You mentioned a man the other day,' I said. 'Someone you used to live with.'

'Yes?' She was alert, I could tell; but she yawned to cover it. 'Why does he interest you?'

'Everyone you've known interests me. It's only natural, isn't it?'

She turned to watch me in the half-dark. 'There wasn't really a lot to him,' she said. 'Not really.'

'Old? Young?'

'Oh, a middle-aged geezer in his fifties.'

'Doesn't sound right for you,' I said. 'Not you. Not when I think back to old Tom in the 84 Club that night and the way you gave him the brush-off.'

She leaned across me and smacked me lightly, painlessly, across the face: 'You're a terrible man, you are. Terrible.'

'Oh?'

'Yes, you're so soft, yet so fucking hard.'

'I don't want to embarrass you with a lot of questions about your past,' I said.

'And yet you do nothing else.' She lit a cigarette, groping for my lighter in the dark. 'I drop a hint of anything that happened to me before I met you and bang, you're onto it.'

I lay down straight in the bed and crossed my arms behind my head. 'If you don't want to talk about this person, then we won't. You've got to understand, I'm not envious, just interested.'

'He was just a drunken bore,' she said, 'and I was between regular fellers, but now I can't think why I ever bothered with him.'

'Perhaps he had brains or something? You like brains in a man, you said.'

'Well, he had them all right.'

'But?'

'But he couldn't seem to do anything much with them.'

'A failure?'

'Yes, a failure.'

'We could all end up as one of them, I daresay.'

'Count me out.'

'All right,' I said, 'well, anyway, I'm going to sleep now, I've got to get up in the morning.'

'Good idea.'

I turned over with my back to her and went through the motions of going to sleep, as Staniland had once done on his mattress over at Romilly Place. Immediately, one of Staniland's cassettes came into my mind. He had recited Shakespeare on it and talked about Shakespeare. He had said: 'Why has anyone really ever bothered to write since Shakespeare? How could I ever express what I feel for Barbara better than the way Hamlet felt for Ophelia?' His voice had broken, then presently he had run on, quoting: 'O dear Ophelia, I am ill at these numbers; I have no art to reckon my groans; but that I love thee best, O most best, believe it. Adieu! Thine evermore whilst this machine is to him—Hamlet, Prince of Denmark.'

I said to her in the dark: 'Barbara? Are you asleep?'

'No.'

'That old man of yours.'

'Oh, not *again*.'

'What was his name? I mean, just his Christian name?'

'Oh, drop it.'

'I had a dream,' I said, 'just now.'

'And what did you dream?' She glided upright in the bed like a pallid snake.

'I don't know, I dreamed he was called Charlie. I dreamed his name was Charlie and that he came to a bad end.' The silence in the room was complete with her listening. I said: 'Is he still alive, Barbara?'

She said softly: 'No. No, I heard he died. I'd split up with him a while before, and I heard he was dead through the clubs, like on the grapevine.'

'And was his name Charlie, this old bloke that came to a bad end?'

'Yes,' she said. She murmured the words through ice. 'I suppose you'll be wanting to know the rest of his name next.'

'No, no,' I said, 'not at all.'

'What are you trying to prove, then?'

'Nothing. Just that dreams can be powerful stuff. And what did he die of?' I said. 'Do you happen to know?'

'No,' she said, 'but I believe it may have been drink.' I felt her body next to mine; it was as rigid as wood.

'I seem to have upset you,' I said.

'There's some people in my past I'd rather forget, that's all. I wish you'd just make love to me and forget everything that happened before.'

But I couldn't do that; there are parts of your body that refuse what you require of them in disgust.

Later in the night, after we had lain stiffly, for hours it seemed to me, side by side, Barbara started talking about Charlie again of her own accord.

'I don't think you'd have seen much in him.' She sounded worried.

'I wonder,' I said. 'I had a friend once, when I was a

young man—Jack. Jack had an elder sister called Ivy. She was about sixty when I knew her. She went to our local in the Fulham Road and had charred for a living ever since she came over with Jack from Wexlow. Always a joke and a smile, buy you a drink. We knew she was too frail for the work. Well, one day she was in her usual place in the little bar that looks out on the street there, and she didn't seem able to drink her bottle of Guinness. Didn't suit her today, she said; she left half of it. This went on till one day Jack, who was my mate, made her go for tests over at the Chester Beatty Hospital just up the road. Well, she had stomach cancer, and they were too late to catch it. When they told her she said to the doctor, yes, all right, I've been in pain for a while, but what was the point of making a fuss about it?

'Well, she went into St Stephen's Hospital; Jack saw her into bed there. There was nothing anyone could do for her. She just lay there in that awful ward, her face like paper, death round her mouth, no strength to fight with; it was going to be quick with Ivy. But she kept on smiling; she was a lovely Irish lady. Well, one day I went into the pub and had a light and bitter with Jack in the little bar and he said, well, cheers, and I said, how's Ivy? Well, the fact is she's dying, he said, it's for today or tomorrow, the doctor thinks, but she isn't in any pain now. I shall miss her, he said, she was like a mother to me when we were kids. I'll miss her too, I said. Well, he said, we could go over if you liked (the hospital was just across the road). He said, I went to see her this morning, and what she really wants is a plant to have by the bed, you know, a flower growing. I said to him, well, there's that plant shop just down the road. So we finished our drinks and went and bought her a geranium, two quid, in a pot, and took it over to her. Pleased? She was so happy! Oh, you are a pair of darlings, she said, what a lovely colour it is. Sit down both of you and hold my hands, it's cold in here.

But it wasn't cold. It was a baking hot summer's day,
July.

'She lay there just looking at the flower. Her spectacles
had got too big for her face, but she was the same lovely
Ivy, really. Then Sister came round and said it was the end
of visiting time because she had to have her treatment,
and anyhow we'd all three of us run out of anything to say.
So we kissed her and cuddled her for a bit until the nurse
came round with the trolley and then we left; it was
opening time by then, five-thirty. We asked could we
bring a drink over for her later, but Sister said in a prim
sort of way not to. I thought what the fuck difference
does it make, and I said so to Jack, and he happened to have
a quarter bottle of Scotch in his pocket and he gave her
some when Sister's back was turned. But she choked it up
and died at ten that night, so we never saw Ivy again.
They said we could have the geranium back, but we left it
for the other patients in the ward.'

'Well, you're like Charlie in one way, at least,' Barbara
said. 'You care for people. Too much so, in Charlie's case.
You're another of these geezers that think too much.' She
yawned. 'He liked poetry. I'll tell you the only bit I
remember—"and now just rest in my excellent white
bosom, etcetera." ' After a while she added: 'Pretty that,
isn't it?'

I dreamed that Staniland had a third eye and that Barbara
said: 'We could dance forever, but when the music's over
you never hear it again.'

28

When I woke up, perhaps as a result of something else I had dreamed but couldn't remember, I found myself thinking about an event that Staniland had described on one of his cassettes.

I looked at Barbara, who was still asleep. Staniland had said:

> August 1940. How that German plane burned! At first it lay there at a slant, green-grey, uptilted in a furrow of the field next to our house. It was a Heinkel 110; it lay there with its foreign numbers on it. It was seven in the morning and already boiling hot, and I was woken by it zooming into our field, throwing up a mass of earth. When I arrived there was a stink of petrol over everything where it had burst a tank. The crew was in there, a lieutenant and a sergeant; I knew all their uniforms. They sat wearing their goggles, looking grim and practical. They smoked, but not cigarettes. They smoked all over, soaked in petrol; the fumes simmered in the sun. They sat there, slowly smoking. After a while the village policeman arrived on his bicycle; he was covered with sweat and had his helmet on the back of his head. He made the first sound;

everything had been as quiet as a church before.
The policeman looked into the cockpit, too, but
reeled back from the fumes. The people inside
didn't care; they just went on smoking in a very
deliberate way, staring stonily ahead through the
windscreen. The bobby told me: 'Let's get clear of
this, son, it's bloody dangerous, the ignition's still
on.' We just had time to run like hell before there
was a spark somewhere in the cockpit and the
whole lot went up.

The bobby said it was politicians had caused the
whole thing. He was an old country bobby; he
didn't care what he said, anyway not to a child. He
said the plane wouldn't have been there if it
hadn't been for politicians. When he had ridden off
to make his report I went back and snatched a
piece of tailplane that had been blown off and kept
it for a souvenir. It was exciting, a really
adventurous day. But the strange part was that,
over the years, the passing of time altered the
meaning of those two figures in their leather helmets,
relaxed yet intent, shimmering in the fumes—time
placed a different and deeper meaning on the
experience.

29

I rang up my boss and said: 'I'd better come and see you.'

'What about?'

'The Staniland case.'

'What about it? Solve it. What's stopping you? Don't you know who did it?'

'Yes I do, but I haven't got a case. What I know I can't prove. The DPP's office would never run for it; I wouldn't get a warrant for my people because it wouldn't stand up in court. Cassettes aren't proof. Yet it's a case where nearly everyone I've interviewed so far helped to kill him, directly or indirectly.'

'You'd better interrogate them. Really interrogate them.'

'I could interrogate them for a year, they'd never break. Why should they? There were no witnesses.'

'That's difficult.' He sighed. 'But police work is difficult, you know that. Especially these days.'

'And especially in this department.'

'Well, coming to see me isn't going to change anything. I really don't see the point.'

'I'm trying to say I care too much about this case. I've got overinvolved in it.'

'Well, you mustn't. You know that. You've got to be completely objective.'

'If I hadn't got involved, very involved, I wouldn't have got this far.'

'Yes, well, it's tricky.'

'I feel the guilty have got to pay,' I said. 'But how can I make them if I haven't got a case?'

'I leave the whole thing to your judgement.'

'My feelings sometimes get the better of my judgement.'

'It's because you're so human,' he said, with a glimmer of amusement, 'that you work for this department. If you'd been a machine like Bowman, I'd have transferred you to Serious Crimes long ago.'

'That doesn't help me.'

'Of course it doesn't. That's why there's no point in our discussing this. You're completely on your own. I haven't the people to give you any help.'

'I'd like to be taken off this case,' I said.

His voice hardened. 'If you come off this case, I'll junk you. You'll be finished, do you understand?'

'I'll resign,' I said. 'I'll follow this up as a private citizen. That way I won't need a warrant, and I can forget about the Public Prosecutors.'

'Now calm down. Let's say I didn't hear what you just said.'

'It's easy for you to talk,' I said. 'You haven't heard the evidence in this case. You don't realize what this man knew, what he'd learned, what he was! It's not just the death of an alcoholic I've got on my hands here.'

'I don't just talk, Sergeant. If I hadn't done it all myself, I wouldn't be sitting up here. Now, you can't resign,' he continued, 'it's a matter of your own self-respect. But these conversations are quite irregular. You must do whatever's necessary to solve the case. You know who's guilty—nail them. But don't break the rules. Is that clear?'

'In a way.'

'Well, thank God the obvious is clear, anyhow,' he said, hanging up.

30

I got to Earlsfield and parked. There's a turning off the
main route into central London called Acacia Road, and I
live in a roundabout at the top called Acacia Circus. It
was half-past three in the afternoon and there were very few
people about. It was a bright day, but that only made my
block look newer and nastier. It is three stories high; I live
on the second. The flat consists of sitting-room, bedroom
and kitchenette, WC and bath. The place is built of
concrete, which sweats in the winter when you have the
central heating on. The sitting-room gives onto a balcony
that is too narrow to take a chair out and sit in summer,
and I go to the flat as little as possible, except to sleep.
There are a few houses adjoining, all new, where men
garden at the end of the day, doing things to their hedges
with clippers they have bought by direct mail. Lining the
concrete road are a few acacias that don't look as if they
would get far in life; that's how the raw scar of my street
got its name.

   I got out of the car and searched for my latchkey in my
back trouser pocket. I went upstairs and let myself in.
The sitting-room was bathed in afternoon sun and was too
hot. It was not a friendly room. There were some sticks
of furniture, a cushion on the floor in patchwork leather left
behind by the previous tenant, and a TV set. I went and

opened the window and looked out onto a bright blue sky, the blink and glitter of traffic on the main road, and houses, more houses, still more houses.

I supposed I might as well eat. I kept some frozen things in the fridge; I took out a packet and started reading the instructions on the back. The contents sounded disgusting, so I let the packet fall on the Formica-topped kitchen table, which it hit with a crack. I took a can of beer out instead and went back to the sitting-room. I felt ill at ease and disturbed after my conversation with upstairs. They knew I was in a hopeless position and were just letting me sail on into it.

Presently I got out the cassettes I had found at Romilly Place and put one on the player that I hadn't heard yet—I still hadn't had time to hear them all. I switched the player on. Soon there was a noise like a rasping sigh, and Staniland started to speak. He began talking about his daughter, Charlotte. I sat and listened, drinking some beer from time to time. Staniland said:

> Darling, talking to you like this somehow brings me a little closer to you. I know I've wronged you terribly, and it does hurt me so. I've hurt your mother, too; when you're older you must ask her for the truth. Oh, darling, I know you're only ten now, but always try and think very straight and then everything will come out right, you'll see. I am capable of so much love, but it has been crowded out by my doubt and disbelief in myself. Though I set such store by the truth, I have found it difficult to be honest—I think through life being so temporary—and that's why I never loved you and picked you up and kissed you as I should have done, I see that now. Please try and forgive me; I loved you so much, but I was trying to do something very difficult in life at the same time.

There was a pause on the tape and I drank some beer,
which was getting warm as I held it forgotten in my hand. I
thought that by rights the child's mother must have the
tape, but wondered if perhaps it might only make her suffer
even more. Staniland continued in a sort of aside:

> Oh, please, God, make her understand; I can't
> bear to make any more mistakes. . . . It's all right,
> I'm talking to you again, darling. I want you to
> know how happy I am we had you, in spite of
> everything. Everyone down at Duéjouls, the
> neighbours, your schoolteacher Madame Castan,
> everyone, says what a sweet, happy, intelligent little
> girl you were and how they miss you. The house
> at Duéjouls is for you and Mummy, sweetheart,
> only for you; the deeds and my will leaving it to
> you both are with Garlenc, the notaire in Rodez.

That settles it, I thought, switching off. Staniland's
widow must have the tape. I brooded about it for a bit,
then turned on the player again. Staniland said:

> Darling, you're the sort of girl that other people
> will live and die for when you grow up—if only I
> could have told you that myself. But I quarrelled
> with your mother too much, and I drank too
> much. I spread only sorrow and disaster among us
> because somehow I knew too much, and wanted
> to find out even more. But I haven't. All I've done
> is massacre our family life.
>
> It has all been for nothing, and I don't care what
> happens to me now. I really was no good and you
> must try to forgive that if you can. Don't let people
> defame me, though. People who do that never
> know all the facts; they base their judgements on
> nothing but hearsay, and are no good, either.

All this nightmare inside me began when I was a
child, after your great-uncle was killed in the
Second World War. His ship, the *Ceramic*, was
torpedoed in the Atlantic in May 1941; he was in
the engine-room when it happened and he was
scalded to death by steam when the boilers
exploded. There was only one survivor picked up
out of fifteen hundred aboard, a stoker, and he
told my father about this. I adored your great-uncle,
and it was then that I began to wonder what we
were all for. My dear little sweet girl, we shall meet
again somewhere, I know we shall. What I did
was—

But I couldn't bear to listen to what Staniland had done,
not right away. I had had enough for a while, and switched
the player off. I looked at the tape to see if there was still
a lot of it to run. There was. Presently I thought, It's no
good, I've got to play it. It was a horrible experience, like
listening to a man choke to death. But I lit a cigarette,
threw it away, and managed to switch the tape on again.
Staniland's voice ran in my ears, sounding desperate:

I had a stab at the great experience, at the truth. . . .
But I hadn't the equipment, I hadn't the strength
of will, I made a dreadful mess of it. I got what I
was trying to do mixed up with banal desires; in
the end I put you and your mother on the table like
my last chip, and I lost you too. Your mother and
I quarrelled too much; we both drank too much.
One night at Duéjouls she told me I couldn't get
another woman if I tried. Well, I went away and
got one and your mother left and took you with
her. But none of it did any of us any good. All our
troubles started there, in fact.
    But fuck the facts.

I'm trying to write again now on a tape recorder. I've left it very late, but I know I can do it, and I've got such strange things to tell. I want what I write to be like a buoy that marks a rock; I don't want anyone else wrecked on it.

Barbara . . . I don't want to talk about her much, darling. If we manage to teach each other what goodness means, she might prove a friend to you in the future. But she might not. Atrocious suffering, but I believe I may be breaking through with her now. . . .

I miss you desperately, my darling Charlotte. I feel as if I had been killed—as if my mistakes had turned into someone with a gun and shot me. I have to try to explain everything in the time I have left—all the errors, the grief and the love. Good-bye, my little one, good-bye, good night, my sweet, and remember one thing—all the evil in the world is powerless against intelligence and courage. Never pretend. Anything, even death, is better than that.

Good night, my darling.

There was a long pause. The tape rustled on, then stopped. Staniland had said elsewhere: 'Why must we suffer like this? Others have behaved worse than I have, yet got off scot-free. My whole brain feels bruised.' And: 'I have taken a terrible beating from the truth and feel tamed, wise and desperate, as if I had taken a short route to wisdom through a mirror, and cut myself badly on it as I passed through.'

I don't know how long I sat there thinking about him, but the shadows had altered, and there was no more sunlight in the room when I was brought to my senses by the ringing of the telephone. I thought it might be Barbara as I picked it up. But it was Bowman.

'Christ,' he said, 'what are you doing in that pad of yours at this time of day?'

'Don't get up my nose just now,' I said, 'if you don't mind.'

'Fuck that,' he said. 'You'd better come over to Soho on the hurry-up. Petworth Street. Christ, why do your cases always turn up right where I happen to be?'

'Fate,' I said. 'What's happened up there?'

'Another of your bleeding Stanilands,' he said, 'and he *was* bleeding.'

'Dead for long?'

'Twelve hours or so.'

'I'll be there in the time it takes me to get over.' I rang off and thought: What does it matter how long I take? He's dead, isn't he?

31

'It was suicide,' mused Bowman. 'Must have been.' He was alone when I arrived, standing by the window in Eric's room. He had opened it, which was a good idea, because the weather was close and Eric had been in there dead for a while. Bowman came across and we stood over him. The bundle was covered with a red blanket; Eric's Doc Martins poked out from under it. There was fingerprint dust everywhere. Bowman pulled the blanket down.

'Not very nice, is he?'

'He was never noted for that,' I said.

Bowman stepped back and looked at me. 'All right,' he said simply. 'Why did he do it?'

I didn't answer. I gazed down at the body. Its throat had been cut under the left ear. Bowman watched me as I looked and said: 'E nearly took is bleedin ead off.'

There was a razor blade between Eric's right thumb and index finger. The carotid had been severed, and there was a thick spray of blood over the wall where it had happened, shaped like a fountain.

'Amazing way for a man to take his life,' said Bowman. 'I never can understand it. No trace of anyone else in the room when it was done—not as far as we can see. As I said, would you like to comment?'

'Well, if you and your people say he was a suicide,' I

said, 'why should I have anything to say? You lot examined him.'

'Oh, come on,' said Bowman impatiently. 'Look, we're two coppers alone in here. Now, I've already sent a detective-constable over to his mother's, and he's told me that you went round to see her and that she gave you the lad's address. She told the officer that you'd promised to break the news of his stepfather's death to him. Is that right?'

'Yes,' I said, 'that's right.'

'Now look,' said Bowman, 'was you leaning on this geezer?'

'I questioned him as to what he knew about his stepfather's death, certainly.'

'How hard?'

'Pretty hard. I don't like being consistently lied to any better than you do.'

'He have anything to do with it?'

'Oh, yes,' I said. 'Eric was a pusher. He worked clubs and pubs all over London. He was chronically short of money, because he had a habit himself. I'll never have a chance to prove it now, but I'm convinced he knew the villains who topped his stepfather. I'm convinced they used Eric to force money out of Staniland. Then, after I'd been over here to see him, Eric lost his nerve and told them I'd been. Eric didn't fancy another spell in the nick, and against my advice he went to see them to see if they would get him off the hook. And so they did,' I said, looking down at him. 'So they did, in their way.'

'So what you're saying is that you don't think this is suicide, you think it's murder.'

'Of course it is,' I said, 'only like everything else in this case, I can't prove it. It's my balls-up. I should have charged him with possession of drugs and held him. But I didn't want to, I wanted to let him run.'

'You let him run right off the edge of the plate,' said
Bowman. He looked round the room. 'Christ, what a
mess for a bloody murderer to make.'

'Okay, but don't forget that some of them enjoy making a
mess,' I said. 'That's half the fun for these demented
bastards, that's how they get their kicks. You get a hundred
cases a year of it at the Factory, as you well know. It's
dark, bloke's got a car parked downstairs, he strips off in
here when he's done the work in overalls and a pair of
sneakers, dumps all that in a plastic bag, changes, and burns
the lot when he gets home. And who's to know?'

'They did it with the razor blade?'

'Why not?' I said. 'There's no other wound. They're a
well-built pair. Hand in his hair, drag his head back, do it
to him, and tidy up.'

'Two of them?'

'Just two. Man and a woman.'

'Sounds to me as if they ought to set up in wedded bliss
at Broadmoor,' Bowman said.

'Suit them very well,' I said. 'They love to kill, the pair
of them, and the longer it takes, and the more mess they
make, the better they like it. And they had a motive,' I
added. 'I'm that close to them that they don't want me to
get any closer.'

He looked at me with something very nearly like concern.
'I hope you know what you're doing, Sergeant.' He said:
'You got any chance at all of proving this, do you
think?'

'A faint one.'

'Well, I don't know,' he said gloomily, "it sounds like a
right fuck-up to me. Thank God it's your problem and
not mine.' He picked up his expensive tweed jacket and put
it on; I got a glimpse of the Savile Row label sewn onto
the inside pocket. 'You want to see any more?'

'No, that's it.'

'You'll have to make your report for the inquest.'
'I hadn't forgotten.'
'I'll have him taken away, then.'
'Yes, call the ambulance,' I said, 'if there is such a thing.'

32

The next tape of Staniland's I played started:

I dreamed I was walking through the door of a
cathedral. Someone I couldn't distinguish warned
me: 'Don't go in there, it's haunted.' However, I
went straight in and glided up the nave to the
altar. The roof of the building was too high to see;
the quoins were lost in a dark fog through which
the votive lamps glowed orange. The only light
came through the diamond-shaped clear panes in
the windows; it was faint and cold. This neglected
mass was attached to a sprawl of vaulted ruins; I
had been in them all night; I had wandered through
them for centuries. They had once been my
home; burned-out rafters jutted like human ribs
above empty, freezing galleries, and great doors
gave onto suites soaked by pitiless rain. Angry
spectres, staggering with the faint steps of the
insane, paraded arm in arm through the wrecked
masonry, sneering as I passed: 'The Stanilands
have no money? Good! Excellent!'
  In the cathedral there were no pews or chairs,
just people standing around, waiting. No service
was in progress. Knots of men and women from

another century stood about, talking in low
voices to bishops who moved in and out of
the crowd, trailing their tarnished vestments.
     I realized with a paralyzing horror that the place
really was haunted. The people kept looking
upwards, as though waiting for an event. I managed
to overcome my fear and went on up the nave
towards the altar. As I passed, groups of people
crossed themselves and said nervously: 'Don't do
that!' I took no notice, but opened the gate in the
rails and went and stood in front of the altar.
Behind it, instead of a reredos, hung a tapestry
with a strange, curling design in dark red; the
tapestry was so high that it lost itself in the
roof. As I watched, it began to undulate, to flow
and ripple, gradually and sensuously at first,
then more and more ardently, until it was rearing
and thundering against the wall like an angry
sea. I heard people behind me groan and mutter,
praying in their anguish and fear. Then my
waist was held by invisible hands and I was
raised from the floor; at the height of the
roof I was turned slowly parallel with the ground
and then released so that I floated, immobile
and face downwards, far above the people whose
faces I could make out in the half-dark as a
grey blur, staring up at me. After I had
floated the length and breadth of the building
I descended quietly, of my own accord, and landed
lightly on the spot from where I had been taken,
whereupon I walked directly out of the building
without looking back. As I walked swiftly away
down a gravel path someone like Barbara came
running towards me in a white coat, approaching
from a thick hedge that surrounded the graveyard.

'Quick,' she said over her shoulder, *'don't let him get out!'*

But I walked straight into a wood that confronted me without a qualm; no one had any power over me now.

33

I had played all of Staniland's tapes now, but there were certain passages that had made an indelible impression on me. I put one on now, on the player I had in the car. Staniland said: 'The terrace at Duéjouls, a north wind in June. Recorded in great agony of spirit.'

There was a traffic jam in front of me, spreading right through the West End. I eased the car along automatically, moving up in the queue, but I was in a different world, Staniland's. The horrible position he had got himself into over his wife and child, and his oncoming fate, stared through his words. Dead though he was, I had begun to suffer from the delusion, because of his cassettes, that he was still alive—it was as though, for me, he was already in the morgue before he had got there. The passage that I was listening to now ran:

> Unhook the delicate, crazy lace of flesh, detach the heart with a single cut, unmask the tissue behind the skin, unhinge the ribs, disclose the spine, take down the long dress of muscle from the bones where it hangs erect. A pause to boil the knives— then take a bold but cunning curve, sweeping into the skull you had trepanned, into the brain, and extract its art if you can. But you will have blood

on your hands unless you transfused it into bottles
first, and cure the whole art of the dead you may,
but in brine—a dish to fatten you for your own
turn.

What better surgeon than a maggot?

What greater passion than a heart in formaldehyde?

Ash drops from the morgue assistant's cigarette
into the dead mouth; they will have taken forensic
X-rays of the smashed bones before putting him
back into the fridge with a bang; there he will wait
until the order for burial from the coroner arrives.

Those responsible for the end of his mysterious
being will escape or, at best, being proved mad,
get a suspended sentence under Section Sixty.

I switched the player off and began thinking for no
apparent reason about a friend I had once when I was a
young man. He was a sculptor who used my local pub in
the Fulham Road; his studio was just opposite. He wore
sandals but no socks, whatever the weather, and was
always powdered with stone dust; this gave him a grey
appearance and got under his nails. He wore his white
hair long and straight over his ears. He was a Communist,
and he didn't care who knew it, though he only said so if
people asked. They didn't bother often. He was a Communist
as an act of faith, like a Cathar. He accepted the doctrine
straight, as Communists used to before they won and
everything turned sour. But he rarely spoke to anyone
about politics; there were so many other things to talk
about. He and I used to stand at the bar together and
drink beer and talk about them. But few people talked to
him. That suited him. Most people couldn't be bothered
because he was stone deaf and could only lip-read you. He
was deaf because he had fought for the Republic with the
XIIth Brigade in the Spanish war. He had fought at Madrid
(University Buildings), and later at Huesca and Teruel

with the XVth. But at Teruel he had had both eardrums
shattered when a shell exploded too close to him.

'It was worth it.'

'No regrets?'

'No, of course not.'

One of the greatest forms of courage is accepting your
fate, and I admired him for living with his affliction
without blaming anyone for it. His name was Ransome, and
he was sixty-five when I first knew him. He got his
old-age pension and no more; governments don't give you
any money for fighting in foreign political wars. People
like that are treated like nurses—expected to go unseen and
unrewarded. So Ransome had to live in a very spare,
austere way, living on porridge and crackers, drinking tea,
and getting on with his sculpture. It suited him, luckily.
He had always lived like that.

Nobody who mattered liked his sculpture; when I went
over to his council studio I understood why. His figures
reminded me of Ingres crossed with early Henry Moore;
they were extraordinarily graceful, and far too honest to
mean anything whatever to current trendy taste. There was
a quality in them that no artist nowadays can seize
anymore; they expressed virtues—toughness, idealism,
determination—that went out of style with a vanished
Britain that I barely remembered. I asked him why, with
his talent, he didn't progress to a more modern attitude,
but he said it was no use; he was still struggling to represent
the essence of what he had experienced in the thirties.
'What I'm always trying to capture,' he explained, 'is the
light, the vision inside a man, and the conviction which
that light lends his action, his whole body. Haven't you
noticed how the planes of a man's body alter when he's in
the grip of a belief? The ex-bank-clerk acquires the stature
of an athlete as he throws a grenade—or, it might be, I
recollect the instant where an infantryman in an attack, a
worker with a rifle, is stopped by a bullet: I try to

reconstruct in stone the tragedy of a free man passing from life to death, from will to nothingness: I try to capture the second in which he disintegrates. It's an objective that won't let me go,' he said, 'and I don't want it to.' He had been full of promise before he went to Spain; he grubbed about and found me some of his old press-cuttings. In one of them he was quoted as saying: 'A sculptor's task is to convey the meaning of his time in terms of its overriding idea. If he doesn't transmit the idea he's worth nothing, no matter how much fame he acquires or money he makes. The idea is everything.'

I knew what would happen to Ransome's work when he died. The council would come round, view what Ransome had left behind, and order it to be junked; a truck would arrive, and a couple of men with sledgehammers. The whole lot would be smashed up and go into the council dump; in a thousand years' time one of his stone faces might be found staring enigmatically upwards from the base of a demolished block. Meanwhile, in our lifetime, horrible pieces of rubbish, commissioned by the ignorant from the ambitious, would continue to clutter London parks, blessed by the senile patronage of the Arts Council. ('The most terrifying responsibility in stone,' Ransome said, 'is that it's eternal.') The dwindling number of places in London parks where you could peacefully eat a sandwich in the shade of the plane trees on a hot day would go on being deformed by stone drivel, bronze and marble drivel, eternal drivel.

Now Ransome reminded me of Staniland. When we had known each other in the pub for about a year Ransome asked me over to his studio for the first time. 'I'm married, you know,' he remarked as he plunged deafly and fearlessly into the Fulham Road traffic. When we got into the studio it was empty, and I asked him where his wife was.

'Oh, she's away.'

'Visiting?'

'Well, yes. Visiting.'

His wife was completely mad. From time to time they discharged her from the mental hospital and sent her home, but these spells never lasted long. Ransome would do everything for her: "She's much better,' he would whisper to me confidentially, '*much*.' Maisie knew that something was expected of her because there was a visitor, just as when she tried to pull herself together in the Asylum Park for Ransome's own visits to her. She would try to make tea for us at the studio, but Ransome usually had to take over from her halfway through because she started wringing her hands over the teacups in the kitchenette, seeing them, as far as we could make out, as wrong and too flat. He would finish setting out the tray himself while she sat between two of his sculptures in a wicker chair. She was as white as they, an atrociously thin woman with terrified brown eyes, shuddering with terror.

When it got very bad she would drop her biscuit on the floor and start singing. 'It's just to keep the fear off,' Ransome would say calmly in my ear—he could tell what she was doing from the look on her face. But her tuneless singing always meant that he had to take her off to the corner of the studio where they slept; he had to take her there at once and give her the sedative he had got from the doctor. If I was there, we would put her into bed together and Ransome would say, as he tucked in his side of the sheet: 'She looks at naked existence all the time, you know, the way we only do with a bad hangover.' We would stand looking at the sallow agonized face on the pillow until the singing died away at last into a confused murmur and she would sleep. 'She doesn't know how beautiful she is,' Ransome would say to me. 'I tell her that beauty is proof against everything, but she just won't believe it. I tell her there's nothing for her to be afraid of, but she won't accept it; she's too sensitive, you see.' The next time I went round with Ransome she would have gone away again.

There was also one dreadful time when she screamed in the middle of tea and biscuits, broke a cup and tried to kill herself with a sharp piece. Ransome and I got it away from her, but she upset the table in the struggle. 'She doesn't think she's worthy to live,' said Ransome afterwards. 'But she doesn't realize, she *is* life. I love her,' he added. 'I could never love anybody else the way I love Maisie. My work struggles to sum her up.'

(I knew what he meant at last, thanks to Staniland, though it had seemed difficult to accept at the time. Skeletal Maisie juggling the teacups with the confused haste of the insane, and the way Ransome felt about her, corresponded to the way I felt about Staniland.)

Ransome would come into the pub for a lunchtime beer, if he could afford it, and talk to me as if everything at home were fine, but it would soon turn out that Maisie had had another turn; the relapses were getting worse, and it was obvious to me that Maisie was going to end up at St Anselm's for good. It was obvious to Ransome, too; but he never gave up with her, any more than he gave up with his sculpture, and his pursuit of the idea. Ransome was gentle; he never yielded.

He never borrowed money, though I sometimes offered him some. 'Good God, not from you,' he would say, horrified.

'Well, have another beer.'

'Yes, it's my round.'

When he was broke he never came into the pub: 'A true Communist is no scrounger,' he said. I had just decided to go to police school then, and I remember that when I told him so he looked at me for a time and remarked: 'Yes, but perhaps you could have been an artist, too.'

I dared not tell him, though I told him most things, that I didn't have the courage for that.

34

I got out one of the tapes to play a second time. Staniland said:

> *Duéjouls.* I remember a bird fell one morning
> diagonally past my window while I lay in bed. It
> was a hot day early in June and the bird, green and
> yellow, the colour of fresh leaves, hurtled down
> with its wings closed for a second, like a handkerchief
> with a pebble knotted into one corner. It tumbled
> skilfully into the wild vine on the terrace and
> pecked rapidly at its fleas with its green beak,
> uttering sweet liquid cries: 'Miladiou! Miladiou!'
> *Later:* Last night I met the Laughing Cavalier
> again in the Agincourt. I don't know whether I
> can really stand going in there much longer, in spite
> of my determination. Barbara was not with me.
> This terrible man hates me. He gives off waves of
> hatred towards me, even when his back is turned.
> It's strange to be the object of raw, naked hatred; it
> glares out of the person at you like the truth, or a
> disease. Besides the orange appearance that his hair
> gives him he is big, rough, built like a brick
> shithouse, as they say, and the very archetype of a
> villain. I am convinced that there is some weird

relationship between him and Barbara, too. No, relationship is too positive a word—an understanding, more. I've questioned Barbara about it, even—the first stirrings of a new jealousy. It was a stupid thing to do, since Barbara can deny anything point-blank—the words yes and no have the same meaning for her when she chooses: 'Yes, I was there.' 'No, I wasn't.' 'What the fuck difference does it make?' and so on.

Because the Laughing Cavalier detests me so much, he has become an object of interest to me. After all, hatred of a person is a form of interest in him, and I repay that interest with curiosity. When I found out, through overhearing a conversation at the bar of the Agincourt, that although thirty-eight he still lives with his mother, an awakening of the answer to the problem stirred in me. The Laughing Cavalier comes on as if he loves the girls, pinching this one, patting that one, always a smile, never the perfect gent, putting his arm round Barbara with an unconscious complicity in the gesture and her reception of it that gives something away, even if I don't yet know what. But I'll find out in the end—perhaps he *wants* me to find out, because such knowledge would give him a good excuse for killing me. Meantime, there is one thing I am pretty sure of—that, in fact, he loathes women and is also thoroughly frightened of them, beginning with his mother, of course. Thirty-eight-year-old men oughtn't to live with their mothers; they become villainous in some way or other if they do. In this case, the little boy has to prove he's grown-up and becomes a bank-robber. The other thing I do know is that, although I am physically feeble, drunk and middle-aged, I do not loathe women, quite the reverse, and he hates me for it.

Every time I tell a story in the bar about my past
which involves a woman, I can feel him listening to
me from yards away; he is with his friends, but a
curious stillness comes over him while I am talking.
Later in the evening, he will always find an
opportunity to jeer at me—even, just that once, to
beat me up outside the back of the pub. But I
watch him with his mates; I think he's a real
locker-room boy; I don't think he could get it up
with a woman in a million years; no, he *collapses* in
front of a woman; the harder the woman the
bigger the negative kick he gets out of his collapse.

   Barbara?

   Barbara will do anything for or to anybody,
because it doesn't matter to her what she does. It's
that very flatness in her that I spend my life's blood
trying to penetrate, and it intrigues her in a
remote sort of way, watching me struggle with the
impossible like a wasp in a glass of beer.

   Later: Barbara has gone out as usual. After all,
who would want to stay in this horrible little
room? Yet I expect her, and beg her in an
undignified, pathetic way, to stay in for my sake.
She doesn't give a damn. Oh, God, what a hideous
fate to fall in love (and for the first time!) with a
frigid iceberg with gross psychic problems and the
mind of a petty criminal! I tell myself over and
over that I am mad to continue it; but it makes no
difference whatever to the way I feel for her. All I
can do when I am in here on my own is to scream:
how can she flaunt herself in front of all those
men in the clubs when I love her? How can she
only shrug when any man—myself included—puts
his hand on her thigh? What is the matter with me?
The whole thing's a vile joke, an abominable
injustice not to be borne.

I lie on our mattress on the floor. It's my
mattress, really, because she is so seldom on it.
On the corner of the kitchen table lies an opened
packet of razor blades. I feel desperate, filled with
the contempt and hatred of others—Barbara, the
Laughing Cavalier. I am a vomitorium; I have the
effect, simply through being the person I am
(something I can do nothing about), of forcing all
the evil out of them, of becoming the object of it.
Through my head run the words I wrote: 'Unhook
the delicate lace of flesh . . . then with a bold but
cunning curve sweep into the throat and release its
voice if you can. . . .' I am out of bed and have
picked up the blades. I unwrap one and look at it.
Suicide? Tonight might just be the night.

But no. It isn't the way. They would think I had
been a coward, and then my whole life would
really have been wasted (although isn't all life
wasted?). No, I must get them to commit
themselves to their own evil; that's the better way,
to compel them to strip off their pretences for
themselves. I am expendable myself, just a rat in a
laboratory that will serve, with its life, to prove or
disprove a proposition. Any life will serve to prove
or disprove a proposition.

Yes, you were very expendable, I thought. Later I
switched on the player, and Staniland's voice began:

I remember the bird again. This time I saw it flying
onto the terrace under the black sky of an oncoming
storm. It resembled a tiny club waiter in its dark
green and yellow livery, flying with outstretched
arms across the troubled dining-room of the world,
imploring everyone to keep calm, they would all
be served. Yesterday I couldn't stand it after three

days and nights lying on the mattress and waiting
for Barbara to come home, so I got drunk at the
Agincourt and then took a bus up to central
London. I listened to two middle-class boys across
the aisle from me on the top deck, talking in the
new fashionable Wapping accent. They were probably
in love; they leaned primly against each other as
the bus took corners, a thin copy of the real thing.
One of them was telling the other about his
holiday in France, and how for the first time he had
seen things killed—eight trout being knocked on
the head by a peasant woman. The other one
remarked: 'Oh, I say! Just like a mugging, isn't it?'

I suddenly despaired violently of the world. They
were our young quiet boys from trendy homes
with bad accents, the future of the race: they were
pro-Palestinian and would always vote for nice
people. They had no more class; they had no more
roots—all that had been bred out of them. They
moved with defiant hesitation around a Britain that
they declared persuasively that they knew. I no
longer knew it.

I got off the bus at Trafalgar Square. I walked to
Piccadilly Circus and went downstairs into
O'Shaughnessy's bar opposite the tube station
entrance. It was dark and dirty down there, but
the Guinness was good. Tramps and perverts sat
around drinking it, peevish faces above tankards
and crumpled macs; two stout conmen in little green
hats tried to sell each other the rights in a
television script. The lights flickered, the Irish
barmen were rude and spat into the sawdust; a
chilly northeaster hurtled through from the half-
open door to the stairs. I drank six pints of
Guinness, which I held down until ten to three,
when I wandered off against the wind into the

gents and lost the lot. My head was full of stuff I'd
seen on the front page of the *Standard* coming in,
about Poland and West Beirut, and my feet ached;
as they shouted Time at three I thought confusedly
that I might as well go out and see if I could pick
up any ideas for writing which had nothing to do
with Barbara. So I walked down into Piccadilly, but
remember nothing except a pretty little girl with
murderer's ears who was standing waiting for a 19
bus with a woman I supposed must be her
mother—anyway, she had legs like crumpled car
bumpers and wore a brightly poisoned hat. Behind
her stood an old queen in a good suit with grey hair
brushed out under the brim of his six-in-hand
Lock's bowler; he smiled into the glass cover of the
timetable and revealed bluish teeth with gold
fillings. I didn't want to see any more. The next
thing I knew I was back in Romilly Place. I don't
know how I got there, maybe I walked.

There was still no sign of Barbara when I got in;
there hardly ever is anymore. I find the most
important question for me now is how to get off the
scene. It must have been bad enough getting onto
it, if one could remember one's birth, but surely not
as bad as getting off. Existence is barbaric, and I
have made the mistake of behaving as badly as it has
itself—insulting or abandoning everyone who might
have helped me, taking a shallow attitude to deep
problems and, conversely, a deep, contemplative
view of complete trivia.

Now I am paying it all back—but what is the use
of that? The best I can say of myself is that in the
process I shot down a few shits—not difficult,
however, if you are one.

Tonight I felt like going down to a ghastly South
Kensington pub, so I went. I have a tendency to

satire, and I was in the mood where I spotted
everything that clumps, trying to draw attention
to itself while pretending not to. Tonight it was a
group of musical youths over from the Royal
Albert Hall. They clumped carefully in and deposited
some instruments in cases on the floor; the cases
were roughly the shape of a bull's bollocks.
Surrounded by these, they proceeded to trendify
over half pints in a very elaborate way, while looking
round to see if anybody was listening. Nobody
was except me, and they quickly realized that I was
fascinated in the wrong way. Why do I dislike
people like that so much? They pay their rates, play
the cornet for a living, prove that they have no
opinions by voting Liberal/Social Democratic
Party, and never knowingly take a risk. They pipe
and scrape away at Mozart with a horrible
willingness and are lavishly feted in underdeveloped
drawing-rooms.

I got in half an hour ago; Barbara still hasn't
returned. I'm having another drink though I don't
really want it. Staring up at the ceiling just now,
where there's a coastline of Western Europe formed
out of damp—soon I didn't see it at all. Instead I
was back in France, lying in bed in my vaulted
room over the terrace, watching one of the hornets
that had flown in from its nest in the mountainside
across the stream. It was three inches long and
when you hit it with the back of your hand it was
like hitting bright yellow, poisoned cardboard.
They're so bloody venomous. . . . Christ, when I
came to I was running about all over this squalid
little London room in my shirttails, knocking things
over.
   She's left a coat behind that she plainly doesn't

want, also six hard-rock cassettes that she brought
back from one of the clubs. Anyway, now that she
hasn't been home for four days, I have put the
coat away where I can't see it, and have scrubbed
the music off the cassettes because I can't bear it
to remind me of her, and am using them to talk on.
When I'm too drunk to write I find it eases my
pain if I can talk it out. What I suffer isn't self-pity;
it is my coming up against the absolute. The
ordeal the writer sets himself is to track down
existence and then, both stripped naked, fight it
out. Everyone experiences this in the end, somehow
or other. But often the contest is short and
sharp—the last seconds of a motor crash, a fall
from a roof, a heart attack, being rolled and
beaten to death in a dark street.

But I wonder if the agony of unreturned love that
becomes the sick, eating sweetness of jealousy isn't
by far the worst?

I remember how I said to you, Barbara, in the
beginning between us, when everything was new,
when each time you kissed me it was like fire and
you said how you loved me for my brain: 'You
seem to lean down from heaven like a wind, and
then are gone in a single gust, leaving nothing, a
hallowed destruction. Only a memory might float
down after, a particle of what had existed,
remembered experience, a mood, a sound, music,
some steps of a dance, my touch on your waist, or
thighs—something that might last on in part of me
and sicken all of me with longing and sorrow.'

Now the particles are floating down everywhere, a
dark debris blotting everything out.

I wonder at times if my best course wouldn't be
to kill both of us. But I am not a murderer.

35

Number 44 Copernicus Court was in a dreadful reddish
council block behind Eltham Road, not far from the New
Tiger. The site dated back to the thirties and each of the
three blocks was the same: there was an open cement
staircase in the centre which took you up to the floors,
and a black iron railing ran across the front of each floor.
Number 44 was on the third storey. Local wit, punctuated
by explanatory drawings of male and female pudenda,
proliferated on the staircase walls: 'Lead with your Head,
Man, Your Arse will Follow.' 'There aint no such thing as
clean Shit,' and much other profound thinking. Anything
around that could be broken had been, mostly two or three
times over. The door of the boiler-room had been stove in
to matchwood. A plank had been nailed across the opening
marked grimly Out of Order, but an optimist had chalked
in underneath this, 'Okay for a fuck man.' Wads of filthy
cardboard, broken glass, flattened tins and other rubbish
had been stuffed in there to a height of three feet or more.
As I started upstairs five Rastafarians raced past me
coming down. One carried a transistor with Capital Radio
on full blast; it was talking about a bomb explosion in the
West End.

There was no answer when I knocked at number 44. I
leaned on the bell, but it didn't work, so I went on

knocking. Finally a big head, a man's, stuck out of the
kitchen window of 46 behind me along the open-air
passage to the flats. Underneath the head was a demolition
man's coat.

'What do you want?'

'Mrs Kay Fenton.'

'Who are you?'

'I'm not in the answering business,' I said. 'Is she in?'

'I've no idea,' he said, 'so why don't you just go on
knockin and spoil the rest of my bleedin sleep?'

'Because it makes my knuckles hurt,' I said.

'Tough titty,' said the man, and slammed his window
shut.

I hadn't a search warrant, and it began almost like a
game, with me just feeling through the letterbox to see if
there was a key hanging down on the inside by a string.

There was, so all I had to do was pull it out through the
letterbox and put it in the lock. When the door opened I
went in, shut it behind me, snapped the key off its string
and dropped it on the floor.

I thought it was the neatest flat I had ever been in. There
was a sofa and two armchairs, a telly with a doily on top
of it, a table with a glass top, white plastic geese flying
across the left-hand wall, and a set-in electric fire underneath
that glittered with polish and loving care. It took me a few
seconds to realize what was wrong as I went through the
kitchen and along to the first bedroom. The windows were
never opened, and the place smelled. It was more than a
smell, really; it stank, but softly. There were several layers
to the odour. First there was the sour smell of a flat that
never gets any air; second, there was the garbage which,
though packed away into the tidy under the sink,
nevertheless gave off its distinctive perfume, mingled with
that of plates washed up in Fairy Liquid.

There was more to it than that, though.

I stood in the passage and listened. I didn't want to take

long over this. Since Mrs Fenton wasn't in, I had no wish
to meet her. I had broken into her flat. I hadn't any business
whatever being in there, and I could get busted over it.
All the same, there was no harm in seeing how Harvey and
his mother lived. I might discover the things that Barbara
had left out in her intimate talks with me. They were not
all that intimate, really. Barbara was not an intimate
person. There was some information I would never get out
of her. Yet, thanks to Staniland, I had an idea that as far
as Harvey was concerned, there was plenty of it.

I finished with Mrs Fenton's austere bedroom and pushed
open the only door I hadn't yet tried. Immediately I was
at the source of the smell.

There is nothing particularly logical about a feeling of
disgust. Even when you have seen pretty well everything,
there are plenty of disgusting sights that don't excite a
feeling of nausea at all. But this one did. There was a bed
in the room, suitable for a child of ten, strictly made up
with spotless sheets and a woolly blanket with blue
bunnies on it. The eiderdown was turned down, and it was
all ready to go into. There were fresh curtains at the
window, light blue, with a motif of characters from nursery
rhymes on them—Old Mother Goose, The Cat and The
Fiddle, and so on. On the wall facing the bed was a big
white card. On it, in black Letraset, were the words: 'A
Child Is Clean And Pure In Heart.' Around the room were
more cards. They bore, in the same neat lettering, the
days of the week, and the space that each card represented
was marked off from the next by clean, white tape.

The smell came from the floor. Each space contained a
child's chamberpot. Today was Tuesday, so Monday's
had excreta in it, and I wondered what the room would
smell like when Saturday came, since Sunday's task was
evidently to empty the pots and scour everything clean.
There was a table at the foot of the cot, placed on a spot
precisely co-distant from it and the further wall. There was

a hard wooden chair in front of the table. On the latter
were various things. There was a list, made out in laborious
block capitals; it was divided down the middle by a line.
The left half of the list was headed *What Mother Likes* and
began: *Mother Likes a Boy to be Clean. Mother Likes a Boy to
be Regular.* It was a long list. There seemed to be no end to
the number of things mother liked.

The other side of the list, headed *What Mother does NOT
Like*, was equally long, however. Part of it ran: *Mother does
NOT like DIRT. Mother does NOT Like Dirty Little GIRLS. The
Only Girls Mother Will Permit are Girls that Punish Dirty
Little Boys Who WON'T OPEN THEIR BOWELS.*

There was more of it, but I had seen as much as I
needed. As I looked at that spotless little table, the desire
to vomit rising in me as I held my nose, I had an image of
Harvey, the big extrovert bully down at the Agincourt,
drinking with his mates—and then the other Harvey lying
here in his cot, dutifully, insanely lying in the smell of his
excrement while his mother listened through the thin wall
of her room adjoining and stood over him twice a day
while he did his business.

I imagined both women, actually, standing over him,
ready to punish, one probably with a watch in case he
passed the time limit for getting his wretched bowels open.

Two women, because on the table there was a portrait of
Barbara in a big metal frame. She was dressed as a nurse,
her hair tucked in neatly under her cap. Her expression was
icy. But underneath the ice it was rotten, merciless, a
sadist's face.

On an impulse I picked up the whip I found lying on the
table in front of the portrait, broke the stock in two and
threw the pieces on the floor as I went out.

36

'Barbara,' I said, 'Barbara, I am so bloody uptight—do you truly love me?'

'That's a silly question.'

We were in bed at her place.

'No, it isn't silly. Something strange has come over you.'

'You mean you're in doubt.'

'You'd be in doubt too,' I said, 'if you knew everything I knew. Really everything.'

'Would I? What is *really everything?*'

'The things you can't stomach in people,' I said, 'the shit, the pus, the septic places everyone has. The sicknesses you have to try and deal with in the people you love. The shit you see that you have to try to purify by correction, the vagaries of childhood, of failure, of old age—are you reading me?'

'You mean like letting an old pouf smack you for money?' She stifled a yawn. 'I've done it. Then you smack him, he has his kick, poor old darling, then you have trouble collecting the money and everyone ends up with a hangover. Is that what you mean?'

'Yes, that's it, broadly,' I said.

'None of it reaches me,' she said. 'It's no more than collecting fares on a bus, it's just a service.'

'Is that what you were doing for Charlie?'

'More or less, but he couldn't pay. Someone was slicing him up on the side already, before I came on the scene.'

'Who was it? A relation?'

'Look,' she said, 'the trouble with you is, you're a bit like Charlie yourself in your own way. Once you get into a thing you never leave go, and I really am tired, but could we please fuck before I drop off?' She turned to me with an honest look on her face: 'I can't tell you what it means to me to have a good, straight fuck for a change, with a man who's a man. Will that do for saying I'm in love with you? It's the nearest I can get.'

'It's near enough.'

'I'm glad,' she said. 'If you were in my place, you'd see there weren't any good or bad people.'

'I've been in your place,' I said, 'and I do see it.'

'Love me,' she said drowsily, 'even if you're not quite the man I thought I met in the 84.'

'Perhaps I never was him.'

We had a row in the middle of the night. I was thinking about the whip on Harvey's table and I said to her: 'I think you're very kinky.' I thought I might as well have done with pretending, so I said: 'Come on, sit up, you cow, what do you know about whips?'

She started screaming. 'How do you know I know anything about whips?'

'You know about them all right!'

'Well, flog yourself with the fucking things!' She went on screaming and started battering me in the face.

It was already morning, and not much later on she said: 'You'll have to go.'

'For good?'

'Yes, I think you'd better move out of here, this morning, and go back to Earlsfield. You've left me no choice. You probe too much.'

'People in love always probe.'

'Too bad for them. They shouldn't. They should just
accept. Anyway, you're not in love with me, you just
pretend you are. You're bent.'

'Well, it takes one to spot one.'

'Come on. Get out of here. Get dressed. Get moving. I
mean it.'

I was already out of bed; now I started getting dressed.
'We might still meet at the 84.'

'I won't be working there.'

'Well, we might run into each other, like casually. Where
will you be working?'

'That's none of your business. You always want to know
too much, you're a drag.'

'Come on.'

'I don't know, some African club, probably. There are
times, I like a few Africans around me. They're not into
thinking, they talk about themselves all the time, and what
it adds up to is, they never ask questions like you do.'

'Aren't we ever going to see each other again?' I said.
'Couldn't we just have a drink when all this has died
down, like in the pub, have a slice on the mat casually, as
friends, nothing binding?'

She considered me with her head held aside. 'I don't
know. I'll see. But probably not, it wouldn't be much fun.
You've come to bits in my hands like they all do. I've lost
my respect for you, but I'll think it over. Meantime I'd
like my key back, the key I gave you for this flat.'

'I'm sorry, I've left it at my place.'

'Well, I'd like it back.'

'I'll give it to you. Tell you what, better, Barbara, I'll
bring it round to you. I'll ring up and we could fix a
time.'

'You can't ring up. I'm having my number changed
today.'

'Oh, be reasonable,' I said.

From the radio in the neighbour's kitchen a woman's voice sang out: *'Just like timber, falls over and rolls 'way onto its side, I'm so heavy and so tired . . .'*

'I can't believe this,' I said. 'Let's take the whole thing again from the top.'

'No, you'd better go now.'

'I'm nearly dressed. It was that talk about whips that did it, wasn't it?'

She picked up a coffee mug and hurled it at me. I ducked it easily. 'I don't know anything about whips!'

'Did you know Harvey Fenton?' I asked her. 'Big man. Takes some subduing.'

'You bastard.'

'He owns a slice of the 84.'

She breathed down deep. 'Just go,' she said, 'just go. I'm expecting someone here any minute.'

'What? A new man?'

'A man who wants to give me some work.'

'What sort of work?'

'Just work. Now go.'

'Is it Harvey Fenton who's coming?'

'I don't know. No. Are you a copper?'

'I'm a man with a mission, certainly.'

'Well, get your fucking mission out of here! And stop asking questions! Always your bloody questions, you wheedling bastard! Now just get out of here! Go away!'

'Do you think there was ever anything between us, Barbara?'

'No, I fucking don't! Well, if there was anything, it's over. Dead. Do you understand? Dead.'

'Well, you make it sound very final, put like that.'

'It is final. Now get lost. Don't you understand the English language? I said out, get out. Out, *out!*'

37

When I got back to Acacia Circus late in the afternoon, I sat down and put on a Staniland cassette. I didn't think while I listened to it; there was nothing to think about. Staniland said:

Barbara asked me last night: 'What are you crying for now, you old fool?' I told her: 'I see existence as a vast tract of land that has to be worked.' She said: 'You are completely mad, Charlie, you know that?' 'No,' I said, 'somehow the balance between logic and desire has to be maintained.'

Later in the evening I tried to explain all this in the Agincourt. The Laughing Cavalier was there as usual, listening with his back half turned to me. He had a sneer on his face. It's curious; he foams at the mouth sometimes, like a badly opened bottle of champagne. While I was trying to argue my case about existence with whoever would listen, he was telling his friends about how four mates of his had gang-banged a girl on the London-Pulborough train: 'Whole carriage except for her was empty, see? It was easy, a doddle! When all the blokes'd had her the gollies dropped in for the next course, train was full of em!'

213

I must wait until it gets dark I thought. I might as well
play some of the Staniland tapes again. I looked through
them and chose one which started:

> *Sunday at Duéjouls.* Just to exist outdoors like this
> after the winter! I sit in the sheltered corner of the
> terrace with an old exercise book of Charlotte's on
> my knee. It doesn't matter if I write nothing in it
> today. One can write and think too much—be too
> solitary, until in the end you feel as if your
> brain had been bruised. Better to rest sometimes
> from the problems, just sit in the sun for a time,
> watch what this north wind does to the land and
> watch the sky, the clouds racing southward,
> elephants swinging into the shape of an adoring
> woman, into a madman with folded arms, into a
> god, into nothing. Grey rags, each one the shape of
> a teapot, hurry like detectives into a black shroud
> that means rain; contorted ghosts, the colour of
> boiled potatoes, collide with the mountain opposite
> me. Meantime the little tributary of the Tarn
> rustling over the stones sixty feet below me
> changes from the colour of pure water into slate.
> Even so, with the storm coming, it is warm. I
> hold my cool wine and watch the trees become
> green, growing. What a joy! For once you watch
> all that young effort, yet have no part in it! Today
> nothing matters; there is just gratitude. Presently
> I'll go in and make a salad for lunch; then I'll write
> in the afternoon, once the sun leaves me a patch
> of shade.

I shall wait until it gets completely dark and late, until
after the pubs have shut. Midnight, or even later. Really
late. I chose another tape. Staniland said:

Here at Duéjouls there is a climate and atmosphere
that I understand. Every element advances through
the year with its own austerity of heat or cold—the
green with the black, the growth with the decline.
As usual, man has tried to stifle all birth here,
but thank God has been unsuccessful in the
mountains—here there is still a blind but true
balance, and in the end nothing is lost.

How easy it would be for me to close the case on
Staniland, let it slide! But I'm going to smash it open. I shall
reach through the alibis of those responsible down into
their throats and tear their hearts out. Back to the next tape
with Staniland saying:

It seems like the other day that my neighbour in
Duéjouls was knocked down and killed by a
tourist. I say killed—he actually died after lying in a
coma at St Anne's for three days. He was only
forty-two. Everyone in the village was badly upset
by the news. He was related to half of it; he had
also just built a brand-new house next to the church
and employed only local craftsmen. Although very
successful in business he had been an extremely
good neighbour and lent a lot of people in the
village money when they were temporarily short.
Yet the funeral was an awkward business, because
he was of no religion. Therefore there couldn't be a
proper ceremony at St Catherine's nor, of course,
a priest, even though the family owned a vault in
the graveyard, so in the end the mayor had to
officiate: he wore the tricolour over his grey suit.
My own countrymen generally freeze at a funeral,
but here at Duéjouls everyone cried—widows, lorry-
drivers, peasants, the owner of the bistro, the
people from the castle, everyone: even the two

officials from the Banque Populaire clung to each
other. I myself felt pretty bad because only four
days before his accident I had gone down to repay
him the five.hundred francs he had lent me and we
had drunk an Old Crow together at the bar he
had built in the hall and talked about shooting,
because it was October. But now here I was,
following the mayor with flowers to his graveside.
There must have been three hundred people
present, some of them from as far away as Rodez,
and I've never seen so many sad faces. Yet, as
soon as we all emerged from the cemetery again and
were standing under the acacias facing the church,
we just turned round in a body and went down for
a glass of wine at the bistro, as the weather was
still very hot. The owner had gone down first so as
to be there to serve us, and did so, still, of course,
in his best suit. We all sat down in our Sunday
clothes and open-neck shirts and drank and talked
about the funeral for a while, also about shooting.
Only the widow, a very pretty woman, and her
two sisters stayed behind in the churchyard, she
with her face white as a wall.

I shan't take a weapon, I thought. Anyway, I hadn't got
any weapons. Still too early, so on to the last tape.

> *Duéjouls.* I remember what it was like down there
> when I first got back from London, after Margo
> and Charlotte had gone. I had to learn all over again
> how to take existence quietly. The house had been
> broken into by hippies. There was practically no
> furniture left, there was shit everywhere; someone
> had written up the phone number of the talking
> clock on the kitchen wall. The telephone had been
> smashed anyhow, probably because there was

seventeen hundred francs owing. I thought I was
finished that time. I looked round the wreck of our
home and I remember how I went up to bed in
the boiling-hot darkness to the squeak of mice and
the rustle of bats shifting on the rafters or whipping
out through the broken windows for a night's
hunting. The bare floors were littered with the
butt ends of old joints; the planks of my daughter's
bed, an old oak one given her by a peasant who
loved her, had been stove in, and someone had
pissed on her mattress, which had been piled
into a corner by the wall. There were mattresses
everywhere in the house with holes burned in
them by the *marginaux*.

Oh, God, protect and save me: be a true God!
Crowns, flowers and everlasting peace for the
departed: beauty and innocence for the dead, Amen.

The tape ended. It was slowly getting late. I went over to
my window and looked out across the balcony that wasn't
wide enough to be useful for anything. I felt strange,
having caught what Staniland had; now I, too, had been
pushed finally beyond my limits, but I felt very sane and
calm.

It was dark over Acacia Circus. I watched the sway of the
treetops, leaves curled in unsatisfactory sleep, prevented
from their natural rest by the harshness of the neon strips
and tilting in a poisoned and erratic breeze. Far off, across
the fake countryside, I heard the mumble of city traffic that
never ended and the scream of a police siren. I opened the
window and sat on the sill for a time, facing into my plain
little room that had never cheered anyone up. I thought
seriously about the brand-new tabulated phone that seldom
rang and the mass-produced door that never opened. I
could see part of the fridge out there in the purpose-built
kitchenette—it was full of the flesh of things that had

been bred to die: processed, force-fed chicken and machined
veg, curry beef dinner for one, cod slicelets from factory
number three for two. The room was so quiet now, without
Staniland's voice in it. But I felt he had given me my
instructions forever.

I sat and thought about Staniland while I waited patiently
for the right hour. He had made me care about what I
was in a way that I didn't know I could. He had framed the
question that finally mattered in the two lines he had
quoted on a cassette. I found them and played them just
once more:

> *What shall we be,*
> *When we aren't what we are?*

I rang the factory and left a message ('I'm going now') and
the address.

38

I decided it was time to move at a quarter to one. I went
down into the street, where the moon shone directly over
the circle of concrete that was Acacia Circus and had
turned it silver. I went over to the car and checked my gear.
I hadn't much—a torch. I had my latchkey to Barbara's,
too.

I started the car and made for New Cross, taking the
South Bank route through Wandsworth and Battersea. I
wanted Harvey and Barbara, both together. I would get
them. I didn't think while I drove; I just experienced a
sad emptiness. I circled the Elephant roundabout and
selected New Kent Road. It was deserted. A minicab
flashed past me—Planet?—going back west empty, its long
aerial bowing; a cruising squad car; an old red banger
with chrome bumpers and down on its shocks making for
Peckham, loaded with yelling blacks and spewing oil
smoke like a shot-down fighter. I watched the buildings
speeding past me backwards—a purple-painted façade,
Occult City, chip shops, a boarded-up disco. When I got
to Barbara's street I turned into it and parked a little way
up from her door.

I got out of the car, walked back and had a good look at
her building. Her flat on the second floor was dark in
front, and the street was quiet and empty; you could just

hear heavy stuff moving distantly on the A20, mostly
lorries going up to the market at Nine Elms. A warm breeze
stirred a little dust in the gutter. It seemed a calm night to
be doing this work—but it had to be some sort of weather.

Barbara's flat was in a low-built house, just the two floors
with a flat on each. I didn't want to make any noise if I
could help it, so I went through the space between her
house and the one next door into the garden. It was
knee-deep in weeds; wire netting strayed in coils among the
bindweed, clamped by it into other junk. There was no
light at the back of her flat, either. I walked silently to the
house wall and looked for a time at the fire-escape ladder
bolted to it. Then I made a leap for the bottom rung; it was
about nine feet from the ground, but I got hold of it all
right. It gave slightly, though; it was eaten away with rust.
However, I climbed up one rung, set the soles of my
sneakers against the wall and hung by my arms, looking up
at her back window, the kitchen. There mightn't be
anyone in, seeing everything was dark. I didn't care; if there
wasn't, I would just wait until there was. In silence I ran
swiftly up the ladder and reached the window. I knew it
would open for the simple reason that I had found it
would never shut, and the next thing I knew, I was through
it with my feet safely in the sink. I felt my way softly out
of the kitchen into the passage, controlled my breathing,
and made for 'our' bedroom. Here a faint light shone
under the door. I stood and listened, but heard nothing.
Anyway, I stepped back a pace and kicked the door open.

Harvey and Barbara were in bed. I saw there was a
chamberpot in a corner of the room with something in it,
but all the same they had been making love, or anyhow
trying to; the stuffy room smelled of sweat and the fetor
of their bodies. Each half-raised on a left arm, they gazed at
me sleepily.

'Get up,' I said. I spoke coldly, automatically, in a
long-rehearsed way.

'Nobody's getting up,' said Barbara quickly; she recovered first. 'You must be fucking mad coming in here.' She made a movement under the sheet.

'Don't touch anything under there,' I said icily. 'Not even your fanny.'

'Listen,' I heard Harvey saying, 'you got a warrant to come barging in here?'

'No.'

'Are you rodded?' he asked in a pathetically artful way, like a conjuror asking a kiddie which day Christmas was.

'No.'

'Well, then you've got yourself in an almighty fucking jam, haven't you?' Barbara said.

'He can't be on his own,' Harvey said to her. He looked at me. 'Are you? Are you on your own?'

'Work it out for yourself,' I said. 'I'll tell you one thing, though, you look fucking sad in there, trying to come on as a man.'

'Look,' he said urgently, 'look, what's all this down to? That thing about Charlie Staniland?' When I didn't speak he said: 'You got any proof it was us?'

'No,' I said. 'That's exactly what I've come for.'

'You'll wait a long time,' Barbara said, 'you cunt.'

'You're wrong,' I said.

We were all quiet for quite a time, then Harvey said: 'Was it you broke my whip in half? Over at my mum's place?'

'Of course it was him,' said Barbara, 'you stupid bastard.'

'You could go down hard,' I heard Harvey telling me, 'poking around like that in a feller's private life. You know that?'

'As if I cared,' I said.

'Anyway,' said Barbara, 'you're going down much harder than just hard.'

'Oh, I don't know,' said Harvey. 'Easy, easy, Babsie, maybe we could make a deal. We could split up the

three ton we got off Eric before we topped him and still end
up mates over this.' He looked at me.

'No,' I said.

'Now come on,' said Harvey coaxingly, 'most of you
coppers is bent. I can't think of one that objects to picking
up a few bob and no questions asked.'

'I can,' I said. 'Me.'

There was another silence in the room, while everyone
thought about his position.

'Why did you kill Eric?' I said. 'Because you both enjoy
killing people?'

'Well, all right, we're a bit screwed up, I'll admit,' said
Harvey, 'but he did talk to you about us, didn't he?'
When I didn't say anything he said: 'Anyhow, we couldn't
take the risk.'

'And we was a bit bevvied,' said Barbara.

'Fuck all that,' I said. 'Staniland.'

'That was a contract, almost,' said Harvey.

'Almost.'

'He wanted us to top him. It started off by us taking the
piss out of him in the Agincourt, but in the end he was
begging us to top him. Pleading for it! He *paid* us to top
him, that's what it came to.'

'That's what you made it come to,' I said. 'And I've never
seen a more thorough job.' I picked up a bottle of makeup
from the table behind me and threw it at him; glass and
makeup shattered all over his head: 'Beautiful piece of
work, you murdering bastard.'

'Calm down, calm down,' said Barbara, moving her hands
like a pianist's, 'what happened was, Harvey panicked and
dumped the poor old cunt in the bushes instead of in the
roadway. Course it was meant to look like a hit-and-run!
Albatross Road? I told him, You've only got to leave him
there five minutes and he'll be squashed a hundred ways
over an then no one'll ever know the truth, specially as it
was rush-hour.'

'All right, all right,' said Harvey, looking at her irritably.
It was so strange, their still lying in bed together like that.
'Okay, so I made a balls-up.'

'Panicked, you mean,' she said. She cast her eyes upwards.
'And after all that potty-training!'

Harvey tried to take no notice of her; it three-quarters
worked. He said to me: 'Come on, be reasonable. Take
the hundred quid.'

'You reckon Staniland's life's worth a hundred quid.' I
nodded. 'Have I got it right? Is that what you're saying?'

'Yeah,' said Harvey, lying back in the pillow and caressing
his red hair, 'sure. Pick up your money. We've got it right
here in the room—it's all old fivers that can't be traced.' He
winked at me.

"You are a stupid berk,' Barbara said to him. 'He is not
going to take the money. No hundred quid's enough to
buy the law these days.'

'And in my case,' I said, 'nor would a hundred thousand.'

'See?' she said to him savagely, digging him in the ribs.
'*See?*'

'You have had it,' I told them. 'You may get me over
Staniland, but the law will get you over me.'

'Don't be a fucking hero,' said Harvey.

I watched them from a distance, working it all out. It was
high time they did. They both had form, and they knew
there were still enough judges and juries, not only to find
them guilty over Staniland, but to throw the book at them
as hard as it would throw. And that was if they didn't top
me as well. If they were stupid enough to do that, they
would both draw life, and do it with the other people where
life meant what it said—do it with Hindley and Brady
and Sutcliffe and Peter Manuel and the piano-wire man
from the Midlands. They would do their bird in a
maximum-security jail; Harvey wouldn't have any potties or
whips or Mum or Babsie; he'd ask a screw for a potty and
they'd die laughing at him on the Island.

'My report's over at the Factory,' I said.

'Just pick up the money,' said Harvey. 'It's your last chance.'

'No.'

'But Christ, you're asking to be killed.'

'No, what you could do is both get dressed, come down to the Factory, and make a statement. You might as well—you're both cooked.'

'For the last time,' said Harvey, 'I tell you Staniland wanted to die!'

'Even if that were true,' I said, 'you still go in for the kind of euthanasia the public doesn't like. And you weren't even clever. If you'd wanted to get away with this, you should have destroyed all the man's cassettes.'

'We would have done,' he said sullenly, 'only we didn't know what was on them. We never bothered with his being a bloody writer.'

'Well, too bad,' I said. 'People like you always make mistakes.'

Barbara said, turning to Harvey: 'Look, what it seems to me like, is that we've got to waste a copper.'

'I know,' said Harvey, 'and I don't like it, and I've tried everything because you know you really drop in the shit, Babsie, doing a thing like that. A bum like Charlie, that's one thing, but this is something else.'

Barbara took no further notice of me. She turned her back on me and said to Harvey: 'Well, are we going to rabbit on like this all night or what?'

'I tell you we're over the top if we do it to him, Babs.'

'Trouble with you is, you've got a yellow streak.'

I heard their voices in a murmur as they sat up in bed talking about me. I couldn't have got out of the room if I had wanted to, because they were between me and the door; I was at the foot of the bed. I felt like a patient with a mortal sickness being discussed out loud by the two doctors in charge of him, because there was no point in hiding his

condition from him now. Still, I said to them: 'You've got
to understand that once I'm dead you'll have the whole
Met after you, and you won't either of you last a week.'

Only Harvey looked at me backwards, alarmed. Barbara
was saying: 'When we've done it, we just take the keys off
him and dump his car. Shame, really, nice Escort like that,
nearly new. Still, it can't be helped, we've gotter do it.'

'For the last time, Babsie, I tell you, topping fuzz—'

She whipped round on him in the sheets. 'Don't you fall
to bits on me like a cheap screwdriver,' she said savagely.
She shook a finger at him. 'I've trained you. You just be
my tough, clean, shitless Harvey.'

I knew that everything had come to its climax and I
moved, which made her face me bolt-upright in bed, and
I heard the catch go in the handle of the flick-knife she had.
All I can say is that we felt contempt as we faced each
other, and I still didn't know why she looked so avenging,
even at the last moment when the blade leaped out with a
sharp snap and glittered through the air, because now she
had thrown it and a great hand had been played. Such
was my concentration on the weapon that it seemed to me it
flew quite slowly; I could even see, for instance, that the
handle was black. Barbara's right hand was now still again,
the index finger still thrust out, crooked, bent towards
me. I could see the carmine nail of that finger distinctly,
and wondered how recently she had repainted it. Defiance
and hatred blazed out of her face; she devoured me as she
watched me, and I had a silly image of my school playground,
filled with similar warring faces with nowhere to go,
nothing to expect. Harvey hadn't moved; the
stroke with the knife was too sudden for him. But now he
knew what danger he ran, living with a woman who took
a knife to bed with her. He was still leaning against the
head of the bed with his last expression on, gazing at me;
but his face was already growing white and his mouth
dropped open, slightly more on one side than the other.

When the knife struck me in the right centre of my
throat, it didn't hurt at all at first, it just felt very odd,
being able to see the handle sticking out under my chin. I
made a gesture as though to pull it out with my hand, but
only in a quasi-humorous sort of way. But I immediately
felt weaker because of the shock; the things in the room
seemed much brighter, and the two figures much bulkier,
more obvious and solid; they had a black, undulating halo
round them. I moved about at the foot of their bed, not
too unsteadily at first, to left and right, not doing
anything special, just moving casually around. I found at
the same time, however, that I could not really feel my
feet now. I looked down at them and noted with surprise
how absolute my sneakers were; I had never known before
that sneakers could be as absolute as that. I was anxious
because this difficult conclusion seemed meaningless, but
even as I looked at them, the sneakers started to turn
darker. The other thing that struck me was the yellow
counterpane these people had on the bed. A deep scarlet
design was appearing on it, perhaps not to everyone's taste;
it reminded me of my childhood again, how I had watched
my mother icing a cake. But it was red icing, and there
were some solid chunks in it that shouldn't have been
there—something out of my mouth, perhaps; my mother
certainly wouldn't have allowed that.

I suddenly felt so bloody cold and fell on the floor on my
arse, half lounging against the wall. There was a whole lot
of black coming up round the edges of my vision now; the
knife was such a dreadful interruption in my throat all the
time, and my hearing had turned into a dark roar like a
train in the Swiss Cottage tunnel on the Bakerloo line.

"Leave it in him,' I heard her saying, 'till I get something
to catch the blood in. It'll go everywhere otherwise.' The
words reminded me of something Staniland had said, but he
was nowhere near me. Both these people had got out of
bed, and this dull-looking woman was moving out of the

room. But she turned at the door . . . what door? All her words and surroundings seemed a hundred miles long. Then, abruptly, I couldn't see any more.

What I wanted to say was: 'I'm going.' I wanted to tell someone that I knew everything now. I had got very cold, and I wanted to tell someone I knew very well that it had got dark, that soon now it would be very dark, too dark for me to see any more, or to hear, perhaps even to know, or even need to see or need to know where I was going: but perhaps, when it got utterly dark, the peace of the darkness would become the same as light, so that my last experience would become as mysterious and musical as my first, so that in my last darkness there might not be the same need of understanding anything so far away as the world anymore.

39

A figure was bending over me like a chunky, half-opened safety-pin. It took me a long time, coming back from a long way off, to get my throat to make a noise like a throat; even when I did I had to speak past lips that felt fat and numb because of some drug I was on.

'Christ, it's you,' I said. 'I thought I was up with the angels somewhere, but you look like the angel of death in tweeds.' I paused and shut my eyes; it made me feel as if I were swinging slowly round a black sun, so I opened them again.

'I thought I was dead,' I said, 'I really did.'

'So did I,' said Bowman. 'So did the ambulance crew.'

'All right, I can see I'm in a hospital,' I said. 'Which one?'

'My life,' said Bowman, 'you might make a detective yet. You're in the Westminster and have been for three days. On a drip.'

'I'd like to know how I survived.'

'Well, you didn't deserve to, you berk,' said Bowman. 'But when I got your report on Staniland and that last phone message of yours I got over there with a squad car and two men sharpish.'

'And then?'

'Well, we didn't bother knocking,' said Bowman reminiscently. 'I hadn't a warrant—there was no time—so

228

we stove the door in anyway, shot upstairs, smashed the
flat door in, and there you were, the three of you, you with
the knife still in you, the woman stark bollock naked
holding a plastic bucket under you and the blood pissing
into it—blood all over the place—and that nut Fenton
giggling and gettin his jollies off on the bed—he loves a
death, that one does, as long as it's not his own, of course,
and the more blood about, the better. Anyway, we got the
buckles on them—her screamin and goin on like a
maniac, let me go you bastards and all that cobblers, stuck
em in the car, radioed for an ambulance—and you were
lucky that the Union go-slow was over, because it was
down in just seven minutes, you'd have been dead
otherwise. Christ, when I think—'

It was unlucky for me that he did think just then, because
his mouth compressed with rage at the memory: 'No one
but a half-arsed idiot like you would have gone over there
on your own, and not even a kiddie's spade to protect
yourself with!' he shouted.

'What have you booked them on?' I said when he had
calmed down.

'Attempted murder for a start,' he said, 'Yours. What do
you bleeding well think? The rest'll come after, Staniland
and Eric—they'll have spilled the lot by the time I've
finished with them, you'll see. We'll have a lovely case to
go to court with by the time I'm through—the Public
Prosecutors ought to pin a medal on me.'

'Why on you?' I said. As always between Bowman and
me, things were getting heated again—nothing ever changed.
'It was me that got my throat cut.'

'On your bike,' said Bowman. 'No one at A14 ever gets
anything, you know that. Your picture was on the telly,
though, last night—what for, I can't think. Must be a record
for A14.'

'Did they say if I was going to be all right?' I asked him.
'That's what I want to know.'

'Well, yes, seems you are,' he said ungraciously. 'I had a word with the quack just now. You was dead lucky that knife never nicked an artery, how it missed one I can't think.' He added with relish: 'But you'll have to be in bed for quite a while, which'll keep you out of my hair.'

'And even then,' I said, 'I suppose my voice'll always sound odd.'

'Well, it will if you don't stop using it,' said a nurse who had come into the room, and Bowman muttered:

'No odder than it's always sounded.'

The nurse rounded on him and said: 'You. You can leave. Right now. You've well overstayed your welcome.'

'It's always the same with people like me,' he said. 'It must be something about the work I do.' He stood up, reached for his hat, and put it on.

'You should throw that horrible old thing away,' I said, 'and get a fedora. Then you'd look like Bogart, only bald.'

'You can half kill this man,' said Bowman, turning to the nurse, 'but it won't stop him getting cheeky with his superiors. Well, I'll be back,' he said, scowling at me from the doorway.

'So will I,' I said.

'Don't be so stupid!' he shouted. 'Just draw your pension and retire, damn you!'

'Oh, no,' I croaked, 'you won't get rid of me that easily.'

It wasn't until after he had gone that it occurred to me I had never so much as thanked him for saving my life.

I lay back, thinking. Staniland would go to his grave avenged. Fenton would do life, in Rampton or Broadmoor as like as not. I didn't think Barbara would be gracing the bars of any more South London clubs for a while, or seducing any coppers.

She would have to do thirty years first.

TITLES OF THE AVAILABLE PRESS
in order of publication

THE CENTAUR IN THE GARDEN, a novel by Moacyr Scliar

EL ANGEL'S LAST CONQUEST, a novel by Elvira Orphée

A STRANGE VIRUS OF UNKNOWN ORIGIN, a study by
Dr. Jacques Leibowitch

THE TALES OF PATRICK MERLA, short stories by
Patrick Merla

ELSEWHERE, a novel by Jonathan Strong

THE AVAILABLE PRESS/PEN SHORT STORY COLLECTION

CAUGHT, a novel by Jane Schwartz

THE ONE-MAN ARMY, a novel by Moacyr Scliar

THE CARNIVAL OF THE ANIMALS, short stories by
Moacyr Scliar

LAST WORDS AND OTHER POEMS, poetry by Antler

O'CLOCK, short stories by Quim Monzó

MURDER BY REMOTE CONTROL, a novel in pictures by
Janwillem van de Wetering and Paul Kirchner

VIC HOLYFIELD AND THE CLASS OF 1957, a novel by
William Heyen

AIR, a novel by Michael Upchurch

THE GODS OF RAQUEL, a novel by Moacyr Scliar

SUTERISMS, pictures by David Suter

DOCTOR WOOREDDY'S PRESCRIPTION FOR ENDURING
THE END OF THE WORLD, a novel by Colin Johnson

THE CHESTNUT RAIN, a poem by William Heyen

THE MAN IN THE MONKEY SUIT, a novel by
Oswaldo França, Júnior

KIDDO, a novel by David Handler

COD STREUTH, a novel by Bamber Gascoigne

LUNACY & CAPRICE, a novel by Henry Van Dyke